Lust Letters

If love makes the world go round...
then lust makes it more interesting

by Randi Kniss

Lust Letters

Printed in the United States of America
First Printing, 2020
Published by SBG Inc.

ISBN: 978-0-578-63915-4

About the Author

RANDI KNISS LIVES IN SOUTHERN CALIFORNIA AND HER LIBIDO is still very much out of control, looking for love, lust, and adventures that fuel the fire.

If love makes the world go round, then lust makes it more interesting.

Lust Letters is a collection of naughty musings, dirty thoughts, sexy dreams, racy notes, and sensual *billet-doux* from my impish brain to my love.

Warning: Have a lusty friend nearby or on speed dial. You will want to create some heat while reading.

Disclaimer: The following may or may not be based on actual events and/or persons. It is meant purely for entertainment purposes.

For ND, a dope I loved deeply.

Sadly he didn't love back but still...the sex was on another plane of existence.

FIRE

Once the flame ignites,
it's beyond any control.

Table of Contents

SPARKS

It starts innocuous enough, I would say
innocently, but we both know that's not true.

"*M*AKING LOVE," SOUNDS STUPID AND MECHANICAL. I NEVER SAY this during, before or after. I would rather say "having sex."

But "fucking", at least in my mind is crazed ripping the clothes off, slamming up against the wall, no holds barred aerobic often in odd body distorted positions at maximum throttle type sex. Sex you feel the next day... and sometimes there are bruises in odd places. Temporary battle wounds reminding you of the heat.

"Screwing" is similar to fucking but maybe a little less manic and generally no bruises. Not the crazy urgency.

"Fooling around" is a bit more leisurely and with fewer crazy positions...and definitely no clothes ripping off. But still so fun, and it may or may not end with actual sex.

And "being seduced" is very slow and wonderful. The build up and anticipation can really heighten the entire experience.

You got something you like?

Want to try a fantasy or some other wicked idea?

Tell me please, otherwise you just get what fuels my naughty thoughts.

A SPARK, A FLASH, JUST A FLICKER OF SOME NON-TANGIBLE indiscernible entity, and then a bolt of desire has stimulated the brain, the body, and the lower chakras.

Whoa! Once the lower chakras are vibrating…forget it.

Sex! All I want is sex.

In the course of a day one might encounter hundreds, even thousands, of people: shopping, commuting, working, and pursuing all the daily mundane tasks of life. Then in an instant…without asking for it or seeking a distraction…physical desire grabs you as an interesting stranger passes through your life with only maybe a brief word or a friendly exchange. Some say it is chemicals or pheromones that trigger our instant attraction to some over others. I think chemistry is only part of it.

The laws of instant attraction could be debated for years. I only know that a certain look, a sexy gait, an intelligent phrase, a friendly smile, or a myriad million other things can cause a simple interchange between two people to become a sexually charged incident.

Fantasizing about kissing that handsome stranger on the train home is far more enjoyable than revising my to-do list. The former makes time fly by quickly, making the commute more fun than usual. I'm looking and smiling, hoping the attraction was mutual. The simple joy in finding another person attractive and flirt-worthy makes life more vibrant!

But what to do if the stranger you desire becomes an acquaintance?

Occasionally our paths cross, not often, just enough to remind me of that original jolt of intense sexual desire. Harmless. Life is for feeling, and some flirting can make a person feel young, alive, and desired. Ah, but now you are entering my life more often, and the desire is building.

Do you feel it too? You must.

No reason for you to seek my attention or my company except to be close to the heat that is beginning to spark.

*D*O YOU HAVE ANY IDEA THE EFFECT OF YOUR WORDS?
The brain is the most powerful erogenous zone in the body.

Seduction through my brain, wow!

Was it planned, your seduction? Or is this just your way…a few choice words here, a sentence there…until my curiosity and interested are peaked?

"I love to kiss." Just a statement you made casually as we chatted. No real importance was given to this statement; I'm not even sure of the context. But this seed was planted.

Later, while discussing personal pain and triumphs, you mention that women often tell you that you have a "perfect cock." Oddly, you did not seem to be bragging, just adding color to a story. Some definite curiosity seeps into my mind.

Later that same night, you mention, "Orally pleasing a woman is one of the greatest pleasures in life."

Now curiosity has made way for desire. For any woman in touch with her sexual needs, this is playing with heavy artillery.

First, I only imagined kissing you. It was nice, very nice.

Now I'm touching myself and dreaming of your tongue deep inside me. Your hotel room is next to mine. I don't dare tell you that in my mind, you've made me cum.

In only a few days you developed my completely ambiguous business only view of you into wanton desire. Just through your words. No physical advances were made. Was this intentional? Seducing my brain.

Only my fear of being yet another woman who threw herself at you kept me in check. I hate to be ordinary and predictable.

So many times as we drove miles upon miles to our next appointment did I imagine reaching over, while you were driving, to kiss you, stroke your thigh or your perfect cock.

I blush to think how many times you were talking and I drifted off to imagine your tongue pleasing me or pressing my body against yours…so many lusty thoughts. I even started to shave my legs daily to be 'ready' if maybe…

I acknowledge the passion you stirred up, but was it planned?

Was it one-sided?

Was it my imagination?

Should our work bring us together again, maybe I will have the courage to find out.

"*I* LIKE KISSING."
You said it as if you were telling me you like this song.

You let this statement sit in the air. I did not respond. We're dancing, very close. Thoughts of more linger between us, but neither one of us has made a move toward more intimate contact.

Oh, I want to. I want to very much. Inside I'm ecstatic. A man who loves kissing: I love kissing too. It's lovemaking in its own right.

An art form lost.

So many just rush to the end goal: sex.

I want to kiss you. I want to feel the mouth of a man who loves kissing. I want you to hold me close, let the passion rise as our lips part and our tongues urgently explore.

Good kissing is sex!

But I need you to want to kiss me so desperately that it builds up inside until you can't stop yourself. My brain is screaming, "kiss me"!

Start at my neck. Then travel your way up to my lips. Let your hands glide down the sides of my body as your lips move towards mine.

I want this.

I want to tell you, but I know pursuit is part of the game. The game we play to increase the tension. The game I must play to increase your desire. I know if it comes too easily you won't value the prize. I know how you work. I've watched and learned not to give too much. Even though I want to give it all right now. Why can't I just kiss you?

*W*ITH SO MANY MOMENTS THAT MAKE UP OUR DAYS, WEEKS, lives, it is interesting to me that some moments escape never to be thought of again, while others resonate over and over, like a song on repeat.

And then the 'what if' thoughts linger in your brain, resurfacing from time to time to taunt you with what might have been.

The classic Hollywood scenario is the sports star who loses the all-important game in the last seconds and is haunted by the memory of 'what if' he had just caught the ball, made the basket, or scored the goal.

In a far less grandiose fashion, the little moments witnessed by no one else often plague my mind.

If the past cannot be changed, why does my brain search for a different conclusion to these 'what if' moments?

Maybe it is the titillation of an alternative outcome that occupies my daydreams.

All week I've watched you, trying not to be too obvious, but blatant enough for you to know.

I know you were looking for me as well. At least I was pretty sure you were. Maybe I imagined it…maybe you watch everyone?

Across the room, across the bar when our eyes connected, you always greeted my glance with a Cheshire cat grin. A smile I interpreted to mean "I know."

Maybe this is the grin you greet everyone with, and not special for me.

All conversations were light and fun. I flirted, at times shamelessly. Far bolder than my norm…I blame the alcohol. It's a dumb excuse. I wanted to, and you seemed to accept it and respond with the same "I know" grin.

Maybe you were placating yet another admirer? Is solicitous behavior so common in your life that it does not register to you as different? Maybe I imagined a connection that was not really there?

Maybe any interest I perceived was just…hospitality?

The 'what if' moment which repeats in my mind came at the end of the week…a week of increased flirting and increased drinking. It was late, or early, depending on your viewpoint.

At four in the morning we leave a gathering some might call a party…but with drugs, drinking, gambling, and at least one hooker, it had more of a feeling of a fraternity event.

The halls of this grand hotel are deserted. We are in the elevator alone, no one around, therefore, no witnesses.

My flight leaves in a few hours; it's possible we may never see each other again. The elevator stops at my floor, the doors open; I wonder…I wondered all night…if maybe you would make a pass? (Make a pass…I sound so old fashioned!)

And what will I do, if you do?

Doors open.

In this 'what if' moment as it replays in my mind I always think how nice you look in your suit...even at this late hour the tie is still perfectly knotted and the shirt still buttoned up to the neck. I wonder how many hours you must have been in this suit and tie? 16 hours? Maybe more.

Doors open. I look at you, I smile...and you with that grin. A quick friendly hug and a 'thank you for a great time' and I step out, doors close behind me.

What if personal and professional decorum were not a factor? Would this moment have been different?

Part of me loved the fact that, even despite the hour and the drinking, you made no play. It would have been so easy, but you didn't.

But it is this 'what if' moment that repeats in my mind.

What if you had leaned in to kiss me?

I wonder if it even occurred to you to do so?

In my mind, the kiss is intense. Kissing can be so powerfully erotic, on the same level as sex, if done correctly.

What if our lips met? Then tongues, bodies press up together, first lightly and then more aggressively. Your hands move across my body, taking ownership of what you want.

Doors close but the elevator does not move. It has no assignment, with nowhere to go.

My mind likes this outcome; I like you making the first move. My instincts for the week were not wrong. You were watching me too.

But what if I had been the aggressor? Pinned you up against the wall, pressing my lips and body against yours.

Sliding my hands down the front, ah yes, you like this. I feel you getting harder. What if I unzipped your slacks, knelt down, and blew you in the elevator like your own personal whore? Would you have allowed this? What if I had been bold enough to try such a thing?

What if something had happened that night in the elevator?

What would I think about then?

YOU ANSWERED THE DOOR IN JUST A TOWEL.

Now what is a girl with a naughty mind suppose to do with that?

I know what I want to do.

I want to pull that towel off and binge on your damp glistening flesh.

Is this what you want too?

Was that your plan?

To tempt me?

No way of knowing.

My mind races with delicious thoughts of what could be as I let you dress.

I wish I were bolder.

But this is a dance in which you must lead.

I NEVER SHOULD HAVE LET YOU KISS ME.

I know on some level it was dangerous, but I wanted to know what kissing you would be like.

You are so cute, and fun, and we have an insane connection. I know you feel it too.

It felt like it had to happen: the universe put us together for this moment to take place.

As we are talking I just start to imagine it, what do your lips feel like, how much pressure, how fast, how wet?...I was distracted by my thoughts of your lips on mine and I had to ask again what you just said.

You accuse me of not paying attention. And you are correct.

I let my mind wander...where would you put your hands...would you press into me, or would you let the space between us slowly decrease as desire pulled us together? Focus! He's talking and asking about something.

I wonder, are you imagining the same thing?

Do you want to kiss me?

Am I making all this up in my head?

If you kiss me, will you expect more?

Will you shove your tongue down my throat in a juvenile, gross way?

No, I don't think so. You are too confident and self-assured to be a rusher. I think you know what you like and are not afraid to wait for the correct moment.

My god, focus! Geez, you would think I was in high school.

We've been drinking; not a lot, maybe more than sensible, but still I know what is happening.

We are alone, as natural as if it has happened a thousand times, you lean into me and our lips touch. Slowly at first…I sense you are testing me, to see if I'm in or if I will pull away.

I start to pull back, but you wrap your arms around me and firmly pull me back, this time pressing your weight into me, placing your palms low on my back and pulling me forward, until our bodies are pressed firmly against each other.

I like it. You know how to kiss. It excites my entire body.

Now your soft kisses become more intense, you part your lips, and mine. Our tongues find each other, our pelvises move into one another. I can feel you hard on my thigh. I can feel my own excitement matching yours.

I can feel any resistance melt away. All I feel is desire. How can it be wrong when it feels like this? I know I'm in trouble now; I never should have let you kiss me, because I liked it way too much.

I feel I will become an addict, needing more and more of you to fill my desire. I didn't expect you to be so good. Why did you have to be so good?

I want to kiss you again as soon as our lips part. It's like eating ice cream…more is always delicious.

Please never stop.

A QUICK KISS AT THE END OF THE NIGHT, WHY NOT? IT'S A PARTY. It could mean nothing, it should mean nothing, but it doesn't. It's the initial spark that set a match to the fire.

Time passed, but the flame is still lit.

Another party, months later…I know you will be there. I'm excited and I dread it at the same time.

Wonder if I imagined the connection?

Wonder if you'll arrive with another?

Wonder if I presume too much from a kiss that meant nothing?

I see you first.

The desire is real. I feel it the moment I see you.

You see me…smiles. The spark is still there.

We play cat and mouse. I see you, you see me, I look, you look, a few friendly exchanges, and the game of pursuit continues.

Blame the lateness, the wine, or the full moon for my boldness. Maybe it's your effect on me, but in clear view from across the room, I mouth the words in a moment of brazen audacity;

"I WANT TO FUCK YOU!" The message was as clear as if I had shouted it out loud.

Your response is quick.

Within minutes we depart to an adjacent, but deserted, apartment. The occupants are still at the party.

Kissing is passionate with a level of fury at knowing time was short before we would be discovered.

Our hands groping, our mouths devouring, we try to quench a hunger that feels as though has been squelched for years.

In front of a huge open window, with the entire world to see, if they should bother to look, I fall to my knees.

I must know.

I'M DEFINITELY BEING INAPPROPRIATE BUT I'M THINKING,
hoping you won't mind; I have an idea brewing…interested?

*A*RE YOU HARD?
Are you stroking yourself?

Do you start slow and then build up speed, or do you go slowly the entire time?

Do you concentrate on just the tip?

Or do you stroke the whole shaft?

How about the other hand? What's it doing?

Cupping your balls? Pinching your nips? Messaging me?

Are you right-handed or left?

Does this banter excite you?

Are you hard?

Do you shoot in the air?

Or does it just flow out?

Do you close your eyes?

Do you turn your head right or left?

What sound do you make when you cum?

How about just before you cum?

I think it's a shame we don't have better written descriptions of the sound of ecstasy.

Moan, scream, purr, sigh, cry, etc.; none of them very accurate.

FYI, I purrrrr. Like a big cat, not a kitten.

It is very important that I know these things.

Since I can't be there...you must tell me about it. until I can witness it in person.

I HAVE DREAMT OF IT SO OFTEN.

I need to know how you look, and feel, and taste.

I want you, more than I have ever wanted anyone.

This is lust.

A lust I have never encountered before.

It is carnal. I am more reckless than ever.

You moan, I moan. Your feel in my mouth is like a drop of water to the severely parched.

I love your cock instantly.

I could spend my life making love to it.

Is it better to only imagine the thing you desire?

Or to have it, and then forever want it again?

Like a dance you move us, into the bathroom. Hilarious…two grown adults acting like hormone-crazed teenagers. But the fire is raging, no stopping it.

Pants off, mouths and hands gaining intensity; in very uncharacteristic fashion I order you "Lie down!"

My boldness again surprises me, but this is a night of wanton behavior.

I ride you, hard. You are open to my lead. I'm so wet the room smells heavily of my sex. I'm dripping on your stomach and thighs. I circle my clit with my fingers as I crash myself down on you.

My knees are sliding against the hard tile floor, as I straddle you. Your body presses awkwardly into the wall, and your head is smashed against the door at an ever more tilted angle as I grind my sex down on you. Neither of us cares; the lust has control. Never have I been so bold, but I need to fuck you. I have to fuck you. Your cock feels better than any moment in my life that I can ever remember. I need your cock hard and pushing back into me.

With your hardness buried deep in me, I come. It is violent. You have awakened a lusty beast in me and I will forever curse and praise this day.

I'M FEELING HORNY, LIKE MOST DAYS. With maturity, do I want sex more? I thought the desire diminished with age? Not true. I want more, but I think it's because of you.

I treasure the moments I have alone in my mind to sneak away for a lovely few seconds of daydreams. I think of you and your lips brushing against mine.

You reach across the table for my hand, our fingers connect... palpable electricity. With fingers interlaced, I look up; our eyes connect. In one split second, I feel you have looked into my soul.

With your other hand you reach across the table and pull my head towards yours. Our lips touch barely, briefly, but oh, the spark!

We have ignited a fire.

Holding hands as our mouths dance together. Complete connection. These snippets are welcome and happy distractions.

"*W*OULD I LIKE ROOM SERVICE?"
That was the entire message, but I knew the meaning.

Excited and apprehensive, how to respond?

Four years of increased flirting and obvious attraction, but with large gaps in time between actual encounters.

I'm conflicted.

Is it time for something more?

My body is screaming YES!

My mind…well my mind always thinks too much.

The desire to find out wins. It really was not much of a contest.

From the start, something about you got under my skin, quickly.

And stayed there…even over the years the initial attraction didn't dissipate.

Often an intriguing stranger can catch your fancy, but the spark diminishes quickly.

You, however, became more appealing every year.

I would wonder to myself,

When I see him will I feel the same, or has time caused the spark to fade?

Will I recognize him?

Will he even know my name? Who I am?

Why do I care?

Why am I being so silly about someone I see once a year?

But every year, I've known instantly when you entered the room. I could feel your presence. People are just energy…and our energies connect.

I turn to look around, and there you are, smiling at me.

Am I imagining it?

You must feel it too.

Oh I flirted! I flirted more shamelessly with you than I ever have with anyone. You drew this out in me.

Every year bolder and so blatant…how could you not know I wanted to fuck you?

Except for the way you would smile at me from across the room, you gave no indication of thinking the same as me.

I've known you were looking at me, or for me at times, I know it. At least I think I know it.

Our worlds are miles apart; maybe that's what makes it fun. It's like vacation; you only get to visit so often.

This year I returned alone. I've thought about sex with you. Imagining what it might be like. Thinking about how I might get you to make a move. I feel I've nearly thrown myself at you, and still you are there, but not an inch closer. Bummer, really. I have a hotel room designed for seduction.

This year I so desperately wanted to suck your cock. I can barely concentrate on anything else.

We're alone, it's late, we've been drinking, I've flirted. I'm thinking, kiss me. Reach over, grab me and kiss me. Now!

Alas, I leave again with nothing but confusion and sexual frustration. And really, why do I even care?

But you're under my skin, and at least this time I've gotten you to say what I've been thinking for years.

Your profession suits you. You can talk and say nothing, give nothing away, and leave people in doubt of what they thought they knew.

One email, one simple sentence after I left, "We should have made it real." Finally, after years of wondering…Hallelujah! I have not imagined all of it. I was not alone in my lust. You felt it as well.

*D*O YOU HAVE ANY IDEA WHAT I'M THINKING?

Would it turn you off if you knew how much I think about sex?

How dirty my mind is?

Sitting next to you, the show is about to start, I turn and look at you. You are beautiful in your tailored suit and cuff links. How I love cuff links, adornments whose usefulness has been replaced by buttons, they never cease to impress. A sharp-dressed man is hard to resist. You look too good. Just sitting here next to you is torture.

I admit, I've been crazy horny all day. I know I'm wet—all day I've wanted sex. No, not just sex, I want to get fucked. I need penetration.

Is this how men think about sex? All day I've wanted to have your cock inside me—all day!

I think about riding you, fingering myself as you watch. I would come again and again. Watch all you want—I just want you inside, hard.

You sit there waiting for the show to start while I grip the armrests to keep from straddling you. I want to feel your cock against me. It would not be enough to satisfy. It would be a single sip of water when parched.

I smile at you—do you have any idea what I'm thinking?

*I*THINK WE COULD BE VERY GOOD TO EACH OTHER.

You love to lick, so you say, and I love to suck. We can fight over who gets to please whom next.

But we have time for that later; first I want to feel your lips on mine. Softly. Slowly. Our lips meet. Electric! Then our tongues dance. That's when things warm up.

You press your body weight against me. I reciprocate.

More heat.

The intensity builds and hands start to explore, lower and deeper, first on top of clothes and then sliding under. Soft moans of pleasure escape unconsciously from deep places.

Oh, the simple beautiful pleasure of lust unfolding!

I want to stay in this place, land of lust.

I feel you, hard. I love the feeling of a hard cock pressed against me.

I love your firmness in my hand, against my pussy and pushing to be deep inside me. Just the thought of you hard makes me feel a little weak in the knees.

Shirts untuck, clothes float to the ground, our lips still eagerly seeking each other, but soon kissing will blur into a kaleidoscope of other activities.

*I*T'S AMAZING HOW SMALL THE WORLD IS!

What are the chances of randomly running into someone you know in a place like this? It makes me wonder if there are forces outside of our understanding causing these seemingly random encounters.

I've just landed in Oahu. As I exit the plane, I'm embraced by warm humid air and the sweet floral scent of Plumeria. It instantly relaxes me. Paradise found.

I'm here for work and *some* play. Hawaii is made for playing. It's hard to imagine anyone on the islands having to work for real, although I know millions do.

Hawaii's sensual nature screams romance. Honeymooners everywhere. And those not *in* a couple are looking *to* couple. The warm air, minimal clothing, and Mai Tais keep sex close to the surface. Waikiki is an easy place to hook up, but those drunken days of my youth are better left as memories. Fucking a cute stranger seems less appealing now. I've grown up.

It's morning, and I just took a dip in the ocean.

I press the button for the elevator, the doors open, and there you are! It's beyond comprehension. How can it be?

It's you with your colleagues leaving the elevator.

Doubt sets in as I ascend the floors to my room. Was it really you? The shock wears off. I saw no recognition on your face, but I know it was you.

How can I let you know I'm here?

Should I even bother?

Would you want to see me?

My mind races with all these silly questions.

It's a fun occupation for my brain as I shower.

Hmmm…should I try to contact you?

I decide after breakfast to leave a note at the front desk.

"Aloha you,

So pleased you got out of the East during the brrrrrrr winter.

Room 808, call if you like, I'm solo."

This gives you enough information. You should know who it is and if you want to call…you will.

When I get back that afternoon, the red light is blinking on my room phone.

It's you.

I smile to myself.

Your message is brief.

You are here for work so your time is mostly occupied. However, you are free tomorrow afternoon. Spa day etc.…and you are not going. Shall we meet for a drink?

Excellent idea.

I leave another message at the front desk, stating as much.

"Excellent idea!

Kuhio Tower, 4th floor has a private pool and bar with a magnificent view of the Pacific. Tell me a time."

Later that day, my room phone blinks.

"2pm." Is the entire message.

What to wear?

Why the hell is this the first thought all women have?

2:02pm. I walk out of the elevator. I look about; you are seated at the bar.

I like that you are there already, not sure why, I just do.

I walk up beside you.

"Hello you."

You stand.

Nice greetings between old friends with big smiles and hugs.

Mai Tais, chatting, and laughing is a delightful way to spend an afternoon. The Mai Tais, the sun, the pacific, the floral-scented air, and the distant sound of steel-drum island music are all working their magic. I feel flirty, like I often do around you. So silly really, but you don't seem to mind.

Finishing the second cocktail and contemplating a third you slide your hand across the bar on top of mine. The oddness of this strikes me. I don't think our hands have ever touched.

With your hand on top of mine, you lean in to whisper something in my ear. Your face is so close to mine our cheeks are almost touching.

"Does Room 808 have a view?"

Not yet catching the meaning of this question...I blame the cocktails.

I laugh "of course!"

With your lips so close to my ear I can feel your breath on my neck...ah, it hits me.

You whisper ever so softly, "Maybe we should have a look."

You pull back and look at me; you're smiling, not a toothy smile, just a grin. I'm smiling too. I look you in the eyes and then look down and then smile bigger.

A thousand thoughts are raging through my brain.

With your hand still resting on top of mine I lean forward, and quietly say, " Whatcha have in mind?"

Still smiling you say "a massage."

I laugh, hard.

Standing, I say "okay."

Walking to the elevator I ask if there is a particular area that I should focus on with the massage.

You look at me, we both laugh.

I realize 'that' was a loaded question.

You answer. "Yes."

More laughs.

In the elevator, we are silent.

What is it about elevators that makes people go quiet?

Even if you were chatting as you entered?

Looking at the floor and suppressing a giggle I ask,

"Are you expecting a 'happy' ending?"

Both laughing again.

You answer, "Do I have to pay extra?"

I say between laughs, "Triple."

When we reach my floor the elevator opens; feeling silly, I skip down the hallway to my room. As I open the door to 808, it occurs to me, I don't know why you are here. It really could be for a massage?

You never give anything away. I find it funny. It suits your profession.

We walk out on the lanai and stare out over the Pacific. We are quiet. It's a little awkward.

I suggest the massage you requested.

"I was half joking." You say while turning to face me.

"I know, but I'm good."

Pretending it's a bummer you drag yourself over to the bed and lie down.

"Shirt off mister," I say.

You laugh. The awkwardness seems to have lifted.

You answer, "You first."

My reply, "You want to receive a massage or give one?"

"Receive."

"Then it's your shirt that comes off." I say with a big cheesy smile.

You lie on the bed, face down, shirt off.

I see a lot of flesh; it's part of my job. Honestly I don't think about it any more than I imagine a plumber looks at pipes. It's just what I do.

But this time I allow myself to look at your skin, your bare flesh lying on my bed. Blame it on the sounds of waves crashing, the sweet warm air, the Mai Tais, oh yes, I let a little lust sneak in as I look at you.

I run my hands down your back, stopping at the border of your shorts. I wonder to myself if you are only one article of clothing away from being naked. I love a naked man, I just do. More lusty thoughts drift in.

I start softly, barely touching the flesh, just fingertips gliding along your skin. This massage is in no way what I normally do, but the objective here is completely different.

Well, in my mind it is.

As I press more firmly, I begin to take some liberties, sliding my hand down below the waistline, to the lowest part that might still be considered your back.

I move to your legs, again starting softly, and then with a little more pressure I work my way up your legs.

Did I notice you spread your legs a bit wider as I reached your thighs?

Was that real or imagined?

I wonder what you are thinking.

As I guide my hands up the inside of your thighs, over the top of your ass and up your back...

I know what I'm thinking!

Did I hear a soft moan? Not sure, I might have made that up in my head.

I continue to explore all of your body with my hands, down to your feet and back up again. I work my way down to your palms, and then back up your arms.

My hands have touched, explored, and felt all the skin I have access to in this position. I know you are enjoying it. Some things you just know.

I wonder to myself, what would you do if I started placing my lips ever so lightly on the skin of your back? Where my hands had been.

It's a delicious thought.

After my lips, my tongue would want to explore as well.

Running my tongue up the back of your knees and on the inside of your thighs: high on the edge of your inner thigh where it becomes your butt, I might have to place a gentle little bite.

Oh, it's a good thing I never let my mind 'wonder' like this at work!

I enjoy the sensation of touch. And you feel lovely under my fingers. I imagine you rolling over, your eyes closed, and you sporting a bit of wood. Feeling lustful and bold, I imagine continuing with the massage, but now on the front.

Starting at your feet, pressing my thumbs up through the arches, along your shins, up your thighs to just shy of your balls, I continue gliding my hands along your belly, over your chest along your shoulders, until my fingers have surveyed your entire body.

I lie down next to you, still caressing you, but now only able to reach as far down as your thighs. I run my fingers along your skin, each time moving ever closer to the center. You are hard. I can see it.

Ever so slightly, I allow my fingers to outline the borders of your cock.

At an agonizingly slow pace my hand moves closer.

Do you want me to touch you?

I would think yes, your body is telling me yes.

But you lie here, eyes closed, making me decide if, and when.

Without even a conscious thought, over the top of your shorts, I stroke you.

Ah yes, you are hard.

I feel a shimmer through my body.

I detect a change in your breathing.

I continue my massage, and in a random sequence, glide my hand over your cock.

In my mind...I begin to push my fingertip down below the waist of your shorts.

I want to feel all of your skin; I want to run my fingers through your hair.

I want your hardness in my hand.

Slowly I work towards my goal; you make no attempt to stop me, but you add no encouragement, except I know you are enjoying it.

I've managed to push your shorts out of my way and you're in my hand.

Most of the massage is now concentrated to this area alone. Abandoning your legs and arms.

I stroke you softly, I know you like it.

I feel another shimmer through my body.

Taking more liberties, I move my other hand up to play with your balls.

Again, without real conscious thought, I simply lower my mouth to your cock.

My mind hadn't yet wandered that far into the scenario, but delicious thoughts of your cum in my mouth spill into this daydream.

I run my tongue up the shaft. It's a feeling like no other. I very gently circle the tip with my tongue.

I envision you placing your hand behind my head to encourage my mouth down to the base.

With the exception of your hand on mine at the pool bar, this would be the first time you've touched me in this fantasy.

Were you getting impatient with how slow I was going?

I made it slow, painfully so.

Anticipation, it's the wait that heightens the response.

But since you upped the tempo, I follow.

I take you all in, oh I love this. I love sucking cock, blame it on oral fixation, but I love it.

My lips slide down, your cockhead smashing into the back of my throat.

My nose is in your sex hairs, taking in the smell of you.

I want to make you cum.

I want to sense the change in your breathing, as you get close.

Do your legs flex? Or toes straighten? What sounds do you make? I want to feel your body climax, and note the nuances.

I want to experience this with your cock in my mouth.

Too funny, I wonder if you have any idea what I'm thinking?

Suddenly my mind snaps back to reality.

I hear the gentle yet distinctive sound of sleep.

It's your breathing that gave you away.

I laugh to myself.

You are in my hotel room, half naked, we're both on the bed, and I've put you to sleep.

Irony.

There is something about Hawaii that makes a person always close to a nap.

I get up.

Write you a note. Leave it on the floor next to the bed.

"Hey sleepy head, you were incredible!

"Taking a dip in the ocean out front, join me."

FLAME

"Because the way you make me feel…"

*Y*OU ARRIVE.

I've left the door ajar.

Handsome as ever, wearing a suit, be still my heart.

You are working. I know this. Time is limited.

I'm a late afternoon appointment, in a sense. One that I hope is more fun than most.

How long might it take to fuck away four-plus years of sexual tension?

Probably more than 22 minutes.

But thank God for those 22 minutes!

If I left again with nothing, I would've screamed or cried or laughed, maybe all three.

*W*HEN YOU TOLD ME YOU LIKE TO EAT PUSSY...OH GOD, I WAS done. Done!

The fantasies of just kissing you moved into complete debauchery. My mind has raced ever since with of all the lovely naughty things I want to do to...with you.

I want to lick all of you. I want to make you cum again and again.

I want to grind myself over your mouth and then fuck until we pass out. Fuck until you have squeezed every last orgasm out of me and you have cum for the last time.

My last trip, whatever reason I was there, came only second to seeing you.

I wanted to fuck, but I'm shy.

Somehow I blatantly requested you to come fuck me.

I'll be back soon, because we have a few more things to explore. I hope you don't mind.

WHEN I CLOSE MY EYES I CAN ALMOST FEEL YOUR SKIN UNDER my hand as I caress your back. Sliding down very low, under the waistband of your pants, so smooth, so lovely. My fingertips savor the pleasure.

Too restless to stop, my hands move forward to the side of your thighs, firm with hair, and then move up your chest, smooth…nice.

I glide my hands up your neck and through your hair.

You lean towards me, a small kiss on the lips, pleasing, but not enough.

My hands are greedy to feel more.

I am hungry for more.

My hands survey the architecture of your body. Sensing every detail. Noting every texture change, smooth, hairy, soft, and my favorite is always firm hardness, letting me know that my touch is having its desired effect on you.

Your skin prickles in excitement to my caresses.

Simply touching you arouses me and the more I touch you, the more I want. But now I want all of my body to feel the sensations my hands have enjoyed.

I want to feel your skin on mine. Feel the weight of your body on me. Feel your desire for me.

I want to feel you in me.

I WISH I COULD KISS YOU RIGHT NOW. I'M FEELING TENDER AT the moment.

Good kissing is so sexy, erotic euphoria.

I want to kiss and let the desire for more build slowly.

I want our bodies to just naturally demand to have more.

First our hands explore, then our lips make love.

Our entire bodies demand to press hard against each other. There is no other option. Our bodies just progressively require more of each other as our lips still connect in a continual kiss.

I want to feel the weight of you on me. Feel your excited cock pressed against my thighs.

I love the feeling of you on me. Powerful. Pressing down against me, letting me know I'm your willing captive.

Our hips dance together naturally. They know the rhythm. This dance adds fuel to the growing fever.

Our clothes steam off our bodies from the heat we create. With our lips always touching, your tongue in my mouth, your hardness in my wetness.

I can't describe the intense need to be filled when I'm aroused. And I am aroused!

I want all of you in me, the deeper the better.

Fill me up with you.

*I*T'S LATE FOR THE 9 TO 5 WORLD. REALLY IT'S THE 8 TO 7 world now, but it's still late for a Friday.

You arrived as my staff is preparing to leave. Working after hours has to be handled carefully, to not draw any suspicions from bosses or gossiping receptionists.

My assistants are worried they will have to stay late on a Friday, to assist with this 'off the clock patient.' I reassure them that their services will not be needed. I will handle this one all on my own.

You start supine, on your back. Shirt off, shorts on, lights on.

It is a clinical setting.

I'll start in my trained clinical persona, matter of fact and all business.

My hands will start at your neck. Working my way from the base of your skull to your shoulders, down into your mid back.

After a few minutes, we'll both relax, you sooner than me.

You will verbally or mentally acknowledge how strong I am, everyone does eventually.

I really want to place my mouth on one of your nipples, but I can't, not yet. Not everyone has left.

In time, you will be very relaxed. The lights in the clinic will be off and only the outside streetlights will illuminate the office. This is much better lighting for the treatment I plan.

*I*T WAS SUCH A CRAZY DAY AT WORK.

By 3 o'clock all I really wanted to do was think about you and drink a glass of wine. But the day was long from over.

I open the door to home about 7:30pm. To the air I say,

"Hi honey."

I look; your door is closed. Ah, he is still working.

I change out of work clothes. Shake off the day. Just sitting down is a treat.

With my shoes, socks, and slacks off, you walk in. You are so handsome.

You hand me a glass of wine.

How did you know? You are the best! Truly!

You lean over and kiss me. I kiss you back. It's nice, really nice. Our mouths always know what to do; our faces fit together.

Already the day is washing away into a lovely evening. I lie back inviting you to join me on the bed.

You smile. You know I want you.

I always want to feel you on me, in me. Always.

You look as if you are considering my proposition, but you take my hand and kiss it.

"I'm making dinner for us, if I'm distracted now I think everything will burn."

"YOU are making dinner!"

I jump up, finish removing my bra from under my dress shirt, and proceed to the kitchen to see what you have cooked up.

Wearing nothing but a shirt and holding my wine glass, I look in all the pots, the oven, and the fridge.

"You have been busy."

I sit on the counter and we chat as you finish your creations.

Dinner was a dream. It's the best thing you could have ever done for me tonight.

A little wine, good food, a handsome man who cooked for me is perfection, makes me feel even friskier.

I come over to your chair and straddle you. Still wearing nothing but a white oxford style dress shirt. We kiss again. This time I have no intention of letting you escape. You know this.

Our mouths meet like always, delicate kisses lead to passionate tongue-twirling mouth sex. My body melts into you as we kiss. My hands are firmly stroking your back, your head, your arms…any part of you I can reach in spite of the chair.

Your hands are sliding along the skin of my outer thighs, my ass, up the sides of my rib cage to my breasts. Our kissing varies in intensity, but continues to gain momentum.

I have been grinding myself into your crotch. I can feel you grow even through your jeans.

Our lips never part, tongues and mouths connected in purpose. I'm giving you a lap dance but I think I'm enjoying it more. I speed up my pelvic rocking and feel myself coming while our tongues continue to dance in each other mouths. When you know I'm there, you pull me in even closer and let me rub myself on your hard cock and stain your jeans with my excitement.

Wow!

I slow down my pelvic swaying a bit. It has been decades since I've come like this, so nice feeling you hard under my pussy.

I dismount off your lap. I've soaked your jeans. And I can clearly see the outline of your beautiful cock through the dampness.

I kneel, unzip your fly, and pull you out and proceed to take all of you in my mouth.

Oh baby you feel so good. I can't stop.

My speed continues to accelerate as I bob my head up and down your shaft.

You taste so good.

My bare ass is in the air as I continue to enjoy pushing my mouth down on your cock. I love this feeling. You grow from hard to rock hard as my mouth stretches to accommodate your increasing size.

I can feel myself get even wetter if that were possible, my excitement running down my thighs. The smell of sex lightly lingers in the room.

I want more of you in me. I want you to fill all of me up.

Once last very deep thrust, I push my mouth down on your hardness and then pull my mouth off of you.

In one very swift movement I'm reclined, back on the floor in a similar physical invitation from earlier in the evening, enticing you to fuck me.

This time, however, I physically pull you by your pants and shirt, on top of me. No escaping this time.

As if this was your plan all along, you land on me and push your cock so hard into my pussy I feel like you forced all the air out of me.

I love it.

I love it when you're so hard and deep inside me.

I wrap my legs around your ass, interlocking my feet just under your ass, and pull you up into me just a little more. You lift up and slam into me again and again.

We are both sweating. We are both working. This is fun work, however.

I move my legs up around your waist and lock my feet around you. I'm grinding back into you as hard as you press into me.

We are on the floor next to the table, fucking!

You always know just what I need, lover.

I can feel you slam into me and stay in, hard. I continue to gyrate my pelvis into you. You moan. I love the sound you make when cumming. I'm so wet. Sweat dripping over both of us.

I feel you cum, our mouths still connected.

You collapse on me. The weight of you on me is pure pleasure. We stay still this way for a few.

"I think I'll finish getting undressed from work now, why don't you join me in the shower."

Baby you gave me the best TGIF ever.

*I*T'S WONDERFUL TO HAVE A SECRET CONFIDANT. NO JUDGING, no rules, free and open to be and feel what we wish. I think it is healthy and definitely fun. But still some things surprise me.

Our relationship has provided me with many scenarios to ponder.

When I masturbate. Your tongue on me is always an ever-recurrent theme. You have spoiled me for anyone else. I have enjoyed this scenario over and over again.

You are talented!

So do all women arch their backs when they cum?

Often my whole upper body will levitate.

*Y*ES, TURNING MEN ON TURNS ME ON. I KNOW I HAVE THIS POWER when I choose to use it. It's fun. It makes me feel sexy and desirable, and we all crave that. This is something that is hard for women to feel and experience as we age. Our society is all about youth with regards to women. A woman in her 40's is "over the hill."

When I was younger I know I had more sexual desire than most women, but not until my 30's did I realize the power it holds, and it just gets better as I mature.

Flirting makes me feel alive.

I understand men and I like men! I like to get under their skin.

Don't get me wrong, I am pretty, but what I think men respond to in regard to me is that I'm smart. I can go *mano a mano* with them. I am not afraid. I do not back down. I look them in the eye, while challenging their thoughts, and I feed their desires.

Women like men with confidence and I think the same is true for men; they like women not afraid of their sexual nature. This is a skill I have honed over the years and use when the mood strikes.

But let's get to a little candy?

As you may surmise but have yet to fully understand and hopefully will appreciate:

I love cock. Always have. As I get older, I am no longer embarrassed by this fact. I'm old school and WASPy enough to remember when girls were supposed to be nice, maybe enjoy sex, but not crave it, along with a whole bunch of other double standard bullshit. This was ingrained in the socialization of girls. I think about sex, like I imagine a man must. At least that is the impression men, media, and society gives. Not being a man, I can only speculate.

But nothing makes me feel more sexually powerful than giving a blowjob.

I know a lot of women feel the opposite is true.

But that is not the case for me.

Having you in my mouth is a treat, an activity I rarely get to enjoy.

So I apologize if I am a bit too eager and rusty. I might need a bit of practice to get back into 'competitive' form.

I think I must be an addict. Soon as I'm done, I want more; I want to do it again and again. Maybe I'm just deeply orally fixated? I think about it daily, hourly, more than that…but I'm sure now I sound sex-crazed.

Lightly I run my tongue up the shaft to the tip. You like to watch.

I love the soft velvet-like skin as it passes over my lips.

I love the smoothness of the knob as it enters my mouth. I do favor circumcised, and I am so pleased to find out you are; it's aesthetically pleasing and the mouth feel is much better, to this cock whore.

My mouth and hand get into a nice rhythm of stroking, tonguing, and sucking; you have completely given yourself over to me.

I am in charge.

I am in control.

I determine what will happen next, how fast and how slow; you are just begging me not to stop.

I love the sounds that seep out of your mouth, maybe subconsciously, completely unknown to you, but I hear them, they encourage me even more, as if I needed any.

You are my putty and I am the artist.

No one can tell me I am not in control and the power at that moment isn't all mine.

I love the way the balls contract and the scrotum tightens just before release. Your breathing pattern changes, combinations of deep breathing and holding your breath.

At this point you will give me whatever I want.

You are my slave and I am the master!

What I want is for you to cum, I want you to shoot it so hard and fast that it even takes you by surprise. You might even briefly choke me as you hit the back of my throat. By now I am so wet, I just really want some more of your cock.

Now glide your hand to your crotch, are you a little hard? Good!

That is how I want you when you think of me.

I WANT TO CRAWL UP ON YOUR NAKED BODY AND JUST MAKE love to you until we collapse in a happy exhausted state of euphoria.

I WONDER IF YOU FEEL IT TOO?
I can hardly be in your presence without touching you. It takes physical effort to refrain.

Your skin is intoxicating.

I'm not sure if I derive more pleasure from touching you or from you touching me. Perhaps it's the synergy of our flesh combined that creates the magic?

The magnetic pull is strong and I don't wish to resist.

Bathing in the pleasure of your skin on mine is a euphoric place I never wish to leave.

*T*HE THRILL IS NEVER GONE.

Every time, yes, every time, your beautiful hard cock enters my mouth, I'm hooked again. Days, weeks, months, even years sometimes, and then again…addicted.

Barely inside the door, I drop.

No hesitation from you, unzip.

Pushing past my lips, you enter my mouth.

The familiar joy is back.

I love it…too much, really.

*Y*OU SIT, RECLINED AND RELAXED AS I PLAY. I'M LIKE A DOG working a bone. I won't stop, not unless you take my prize away. You sip wine as I lick, suck, and relish. I feel your heat, you harden, and I stop.

I don't want you to cum, not yet, because then it will be over. You will slip back to your life.

Tomorrow as I travel, I will be consumed by my thoughts of your cock. How will I be able to get it back again to play?

The cravings will take weeks to diminish. For this I both hate and love you.

I WOKE WITH THE SLIGHT TASTE OF YOUR CUM IN MY MOUTH.
I smiled.

It's going to be a wonderful day.

"**O**H WHAT A NIGHT...LATE **D**ECEMBER BACK IN.... **O**H WHAT A very special time for me..."

"And it ended much too soon, oh what...what a night...I was never going to be the same, what a...what a night..."

Like the melody of a tune that lingers in your head, and you find yourself humming even though you don't know all the word... even so, you hum it out loud and smile. Your late-night visit makes me hum happily.

It feels like a dream...in the morning it's difficult to believe so much happened and it was real, no, a fantasyland I visited in my sleep.

With so much expectation, and still really no expectations, you came through the door, tired, stressed, hungry, and very handsome. I was nervous for many reasons. I think it's normal to be excited-nervous the first time. We both knew what would happen, but still, normal insecurities entered my brain. "I wonder if I don't excite him, " or "what if" we are not compatible in bed." Or any of a thousand other thoughts scrambled through my mind.

"Lie down. Let me try to rub some of the stresses away."

You collapse on the bed.

I untuck your dress shirt and massage your back, your arms, your neck, and your ass. You are still talking a million words per minute about all the details of the day and week. You're not really talking to me, just letting off steam, built up from such a busy day.

I listen.

Massaging you is good for both of us. You calm down and I relax. Let things unfold in a relaxed, gentle way.

I glide my hand under your shirt. Skin-on-skin contact. I like that and so do you, I can tell. I slide my hands down the backside of your trousers, ahhh more skin, and you without underwear. I slide my hand down your entire ass cheek. I like your skin already. And I know you like me touching you; I can tell because you slow your speech down and words are no longer pouring out of you.

You roll over on your back. We kiss. It's nice, really nice. No need to rush, we know where it's going. We continue, bodies pressing up against each other, hands exploring, first over clothes, and then onto skin. It is all so nice.

No awkwardness at all while clothes begin to disappear until it's just skin on skin, and that is always my favorite. We are still kissing, it's deeper and more intense, but still so nice.

You begin your descent down my body. First kisses on neck, oh how I love that, to my breasts and my nipples. My skin is on high alert. Every placement of your lips makes me shimmer. Oh yes, I'm aroused. We can both smell sex.

I'm very excited, but still apprehensive. I love cunnilingus, but it is so intimate, so personal. It's hard to relax. Letting you be where I can't even see. So vulnerable, but oh, it feels so good, my new lover.

Pleasing orally is a favorite of yours and mine. For months you have asked to lick me and for months I have waited for tonight.

Very delicately your lips brush up against my pussy. I already know in that moment that this will be a night I will always remember.

Your tongue circles my outer folds. Ah, lover, you know what you are doing, and I love you for it.

You raise your head up, look at me, and tell me how much you love my pussy.

I think at that point you could have asked for anything, and I would have said yes.

You grab a pillow, I raise my hips up, and then you dive in. I'm sure no one in my life has ever loved licking me as much as you.

Licking, tongue fucking, sucking, biting…all so wonderful. Fast, slow, hard, soft…so incredible! But you sent me to another plane of consciousness while lapping my clit, like you were painting a fence with your tongue. Pure pleasure.

I ground my pelvis on your mouth and tongue, but you came back with even more intensity, moving with every convolution of my body as I came on your face again, for the third or fourth time.

Even after that, you kept your tongue on me, gently at first, and again building the intensity until I climaxed again for who knows how many times. Your tongue gave me one of the truly best sexual experiences of my life. You are a god of lingual loving.

With our bodies pressed tight against each other you still kept me going with your fingers. I came again while you held me. I felt we were like one person.

Finally, you entered me. I was so wet and open for you, I'm sure you slid in like a hot knife through soft butter.

Moving together like we had been dance partners for years… first slowly and then pounding…legs, arms, bodies, and tongues wrapped up together to create one unit of sexual energy. It was so beautiful. Even now my body remembers the tiniest of details.

Using the head of your dick to rub myself to yet another orgasm, and you slamming your hardness into me just as I was peaking.

So many little details to savor of a magnificent evening, night, and morning, your talented tongue on me for hours will forever be engrained as a fantasyland I will think I dreamt.

Oh it was so magical, my love.

"Oh what a night!…"

*Y*OU LOOK SO BEAUTIFUL LYING THERE SLEEPING, NAKED and perfect.

*A*s GROWN-UPS WE DON'T LET OUR MINDS WANDER INTO daydreams as much as we should, too busy getting all the necessary chores of each day accomplished to allow for such frivolities.

In my few free seconds of unoccupied time, my mind always drifts to you. Each minute spent with you is worthy of hours of erotic daydreams.

After hours of passion, we are both spent. Lying on top of me, our bodies cradling each other. Arms and legs entwine together so tight we form a cocoon. Bonding closeness after sharing so much physical and emotional love. Taking each other to the edge and now resting from the journey.

Your cock is resting between my legs. Thinking there can be no more tonight, we have exhausted our reserves four times over. But the feel of you pressing against my lower lips causes my desire for you to stir yet again. I'm insatiable tonight. You make me feel this wanton desire.

I reach down between our bodies, surprised but not ashamed at my boldness, and take hold of you. You are soft but lovely. Having already given so much in one night, I know arousing you at this time would be nearly physically impossible.

But you have unveiled the greedy sex goddess and the feel of you, even in your spent state, makes me want more still.

I take hold of you, my toy, and begin to rub the head against my lips. Ah yes, you excite me. Brazen behavior even after all we have shared tonight. I use you as my human dildo.

I rub your head against my lips circling my clit with the tip. And it feels incredible. Getting more and more excited I feel my body responding. My wetness increases, supplying lubricant for my masturbation. Surprisingly, your body responds and I feel you getting harder as I rub your cock on my clit.

Amazingly, after hours of passion we can be aroused to this level, yet again. But I feel you harden and I respond by using your hardness to concentrate on my point of pleasure.

Our hips are pressing into each other in a nice fucking rhythm. You are solid now. I feel selfish to continue using all this hardness to masturbate myself. But I'm so close to coming yet again that I hoard your cock all for my pleasure.

My body starts to tense, my head rolls back, I gasp in pleasure; you know I'm seconds away. At the exact moment you tell me

"put me at your opening"…

Oh god, I had no idea I could feel any more pleasure, I do as you slam your concrete hardness into me with so much force I feel my breath pushed out of my body and we move as a unit.

The intensity of having you in me escalates my coming to an entirely different plane. How is it possible to feel so much, still, after all the hours of pleasure?

You slam me hard again and again. I guess it's your turn after I used you as my toy and had my way with your cock.

But with every fuck, I feel it deep at my core. Primal pleasure is beginning to bubble up to the surface. You are mining deep into my sex at a place of pure pleasure. All id, per Freud.

Fuck me!

Oh god, please just fuck me harder.

I can't verbalize this thought, I'm beyond words, but my body is screaming it to you. And you hear me.

Our bodies slam against each other, sweat beading on our collective flesh. A sound foreign to myself escapes my lips, it is from someplace deep, and you fuck me even harder and faster. My arms, legs, and hands claw at you to pull even more of you into me. We crash into each other until we are one.

Sweet exhaustion!

*W*HEN YOU MOVED YOUR FINGERS WET FROM ME TO YOUR mouth, oh my! That was deeply erotic, my friend.

*M*ESSAGE FROM YOU:

"You think you can get two out of me?"

My response:

"Three."

You:

"That would be something."

Me:

"Rest up."

*W*E'RE DRIVING, WE'RE RUNNING LATE, AND WE ARE BOTH horny.

So much of life is in the car. Trying to multitask, we eat, primp, talk, and sleep...it only seems logical that, in time, we try sex. Probably not the safest activity, but it was fun trying.

*D*URING THE SUMMER, DROVES OF PEOPLE STORM THE BEACHES during the day, but it is at night when I like to go.

I have always had a thing for the ocean, especially at night.

I love the sounds of the waves crashing, the salty warm air, and the dazzling moon on the water.

The warm night air and the water are a natural aphrodisiac.

The ocean at night always puts me in 'the mood.'

I was so happy when you suggested we meet at our lifeguard tower. I know it well. It stands all the way at the end, very quiet and deserted.

We sit down, hanging our feet over the edge of the tower platform. Chatting, drinking, and watching the waves crash by starlight.

We both know why we are there and what is going to happen, but it's nice to catch up on life and let the wine have its desired effect.

We kiss, always nice.

There is always immediate heat when our lips touch. First lips, then tongues, I love to kiss and so do you.

We both get so turned on by kissing; it is a shame we have to stop sometimes to fuck, depending on our position of choice.

I know what position you want tonight. And I've been in a heightened state of arousal all day. Damp down there, all day. Giving off the pheromones of sex to anyone paying any attention.

Discovered by accident, but we both love fucking to the sound and smell of the ocean. The lifeguard tower means doggie style so we can both face the powerful vastness of the Pacific.

Your hand moves down the front of my chest; my nipples know you are near. You glide your hand over them, and I feel my breath shorten for an instant. I start to stroke your crotch. I try to resist, but I can never stay away very long. Your cock is what I want. You know this. I know this. It's been too long, and I can't wait. I'm too impatient; I want you to fuck me to the sound of crashing waves.

You turn me around. We are both facing the ocean. You glide your hands over the front of my body. Your lips and tongue are nibbling on the side of my neck. Nothing weakens me faster. There is a direct line from the base of my neck to my snatch. It puts me in a dreamy sex state.

You whisper, "bend over" while pressing on my back. My ass is pushing against your crotch. My arms are resting on the railing. You raise my skirt and rub your hands across my bare skin. You instruct me to "bend over farther."

I reach my hands to the wood planks below my feet, unsure of why I need to be this far over, when I feel you.

But it's not your cock, as expected, it's soft and warm. Your tongue is lapping at my opening.

You surprised me in the most wonderful way.

I'm flexed at the waist, fingers resting on my feet, listening to the sound of the ocean as you lick me from behind.

Your nose pushes into my ass, rimming me a few times, and then you are working your tongue down my folds into my opening and circling my clit. I love when you lick me, and surprising me from behind is a euphoric treat. I just let myself relax and enjoy you tasting me.

Lover, you are always full of the best surprises!

I am wet, really wet, and the breeze off the ocean makes me aware of my dampness even more, causing a chill when you remove the warmth of your lips away from me. The sweet smell of my pussy lingers in the salty ocean air.

You stand. In one thrust you enter me.

I love this!

Your hardness is forcing, pushing inside deeper, as the waves crash on the sand.

I rise up and rest my arms on the upper railing for support and use it to counterbalance the force of our bodies smashing against each other.

You push yourself into me as hard as I press back into you. Crashing. Slapping our flesh.

Yes, lover, "Fuck me!"

Slam into me!

Let me feel the power in your cock!

You grab the top of my hips, pulling me into you even harder. Yes, this is fucking.

I grind myself back to meet each charge. With every thrust I feel a deep tingling spread across my body, building slowly, and moving closer and closer.

You are pounding an orgasm out of me. You plan to crash your cock into me until I can't help but cum.

The breeze off the ocean makes me aware of my wetness trickling down my inner thighs.

You continue your surge, fucking me hard, fucking until you've pounded me to a point of elation. I feel it, the point where you can't stop. Powerful waves of pleasure sweep over my entire being. No one, nothing can stop it. My body tenses and relaxes; at the same time from deep within, the shudder moves out of my body until I scream!

Yes! Yes! Yes!

OH GOD YES!

No one can hear my shouts of ecstasy. The ocean absorbs all sounds.

Yes, lover, I love ocean sex.

*C*AN YOU FEEL MY TONGUE CIRCLING THE TIP OF YOUR COCK?
Just before I take you all the way down my throat?

I know you can envision it, because you like to watch.

You always watch when I'm enjoying you in my mouth.

I've glanced up and seen you watching.

Are you getting hard?

Good.

Take your hand and rub it across the front of your pants and tell me what you are thinking.

I'll be here waiting...

"so, hello"

"hello"

"Talking to you makes me want to put my hands down my pants and feel how hard your voice makes me."

This makes me want to drop the phone and head to you to feel for myself.

*G*OT HOME VERY LATE LAST NIGHT, LIKE MANY NIGHTS...NATURE of the beast. And had to wake very early, like always.

But I was fortunate enough to have a little break in my day. So I snuck in a little nap after I fingered myself to two very nice orgasms.

Any idea what I thought about?

You.

I thought about how wonderful you make me feel.

I was just lying back and enjoying your tongue lapping at my pussy.

I love it.

It makes me weak, just thinking about your mouth on me.

Long strokes, short ones, fast, slow, circling my clit, and sucking it. Hard tonguing, and then soft.

You have a talent for combining all the skills in a wonderful blissful intense experience.

I'm a lucky girl.

I admit I was lazy. I just lay there and let you lick me while I had orgasm after orgasm.

I was too paralyzed by pleasure.

I'm not sure I could have moved if I wanted to. I just exist... falling deeper and deeper into ecstasy.

Finally I passed out and woke up very happy lady...and very relaxed.

You are a true talent.

*T*ELL ME SOMETHING THAT EXCITES YOU.

"You know what I like."

Do I?

Ok, I know a few things, but there is so much more to discover.

You like smooth and hairless, which I'm happy to accommodate because you enjoy licking me, which I love beyond question. My lust level increased substantially when I found this out.

I lose respect and romantic interest in men who won't. (Stupid little boys: you'll understand what I mean, little boys, when you grow up and learn to love the entirety of a woman's body.)

I'm wet just thinking about you between my legs. It was a challenge, I wanted to come on your tongue, but I always want to watch you eating me, so I can get myself off later as I envision you lapping my pussy. I wanted to engrave every detail in my cortex. My pleasure state and mental cognition fight each other.

Your perfect hair, sprinkled with gray, between my thighs. An image that always excites me. Your mouth sucking on my cunt, your tongue everywhere…working very low, then sliding up to my clit…ah yes!

You want anything from me…ask me now…I would say yes to anything.

You look so good eating my pussy. It makes me want to have you fuck me. I have sex A.D.D.

Wonder if I rode your face? Would you like that?

Grinding my pussy on your tongue and mouth. You know how wet you make me. Your face would be glazed with my excitement. Good thing I smell and taste delicious. I'll have to find out; the idea is sending bolts of electricity through my body.

How about if I slide down and ride your cock?

Not all men like the woman on top. They need to do the fucking, but would you like me to fuck you? Move my hips up and down and around your cock? I could lean way back so you can see how shiny I make your dick as you slide in and out. I'll play with my clit until I come with your cock buried in me while you watch.

Does this excite you?

We both like your cock in my mouth, not sure who likes it more. I know you like it fast, but how about hard versus soft?

How about if I suck on your balls?

How about lower?

There are things I don't know about you, lover. Things I want to find out.

But I'm not good at 69. I can't focus on both very well. I'm 100 percent giving or 100 percent receiving. I'm a myopic lover, perhaps.

*Y*OU INQUIRED ABOUT WHAT EXCITES ME.

For as long as I can remember, I've gotten incredibly horny when in a library. Maybe because the first boy I ever really liked kissed me in a library. Add to this the fact that you are supposed to be mouse-quiet, and the thrill of getting caught becomes especially titillating. After all, libraries are places for scholarly thoughts, not lusty ideas which seem naughty, if not forbidden, in such a staid place.

I have attended many universities, and every library I have ever studied in…stimulated me. To the point that I can't even study, all I think about is sex.

I've quietly gotten off more than once down in the secluded study areas with no one around: just me, my randy brain, and thousands of books. I had to…or I would never have been able to study. I simply could not concentrate on anything else.

I'm sure this is a crime of some kind, if I were ever to be caught. The local headlines would be hilarious trying to state the facts of this misdemeanor in as delicate a fashion as possible. Maybe it would just be downgraded to a "lewd act in public." That would be boring news copy.

So when you ask me what excites me…I would love to get you between the book stacks.

We'll casually walk about the library, until we find a very desert-ed location. The thrill of being so impish in such a scholarly place is exciting.

I've fantasized countless times of being licked while reading at a large wooden communal study desk by a tongue-talented boy under the table.

We'll start like teenagers by making out between the rows of books. Our hands explore our bodies. I simply can't help myself. I'll break away to slide down to my knees and unzip your pants. Extract my treasure.

Every time it excites me.

I stroke you, you are hard, but you are about to get harder.

I plant my mouth over the tip and glide my lips down to the base, very deep. I hear you gasp a moan.

You like it and I love it.

I whisper with a smile, "Quiet, you are in a library."

I slide my lips back to the top, circle my tongue along the ridge, and then slide down to the base again; this time deeper and with a little more pressure, you moan again.

"Quiet, baby, or we will get caught."

I know you like it, and I'm so turned on now I couldn't stop if I had to.

Your cock in my mouth, bracing yourself between the books, is a fantasy come true.

I continue to glide my mouth, lips, and tongue up and down. This action is hypnotic to me.

I use one hand to move in unison with my mouth and the other to cup your balls, and at times to grab your ass to pull you deeper into my mouth.

You push yourself deeper into me as I suck all of you in. I run my tongue along the shaft and back up to the tip, never letting you leave my mouth.

Your legs begin to tremble; you are so hard in my mouth. I love this.

In my mind, I tell you to shoot your cum down my throat. I can't talk now…I'm too busy.

I want it all!

You moan too loud and push yourself into me and pull my head down on you a little deeper.

I suck. I suck until I know I've gotten every drop.

A few seconds pass, and I awaken from my blow job delirium and realize where we are.

I stand up, you zip up, and not more than 5 seconds later the elderly librarian walks down our book stack with a blush in her cheeks.

We quickly head for the exit, trying not to giggle in the library as we make our way out the front door.

Tell me something that excites you.

WE SNEAK BACK TO THE HOTEL TO RELAX BEFORE WE START the night's activities. Before we even get in the room, in the elevator, you reach up the side of my white shorts and caress me through my panties, gently massaging. I open my stance wider. Thank God we're staying on a high floor. We have plenty of time. You are searching for the first wetness and you find it.

We back up against the wall and the elevator stops.

We're stuck.

We use the intercom. They tell us not to worry. No danger, but it's gonna be about a half an hour before they can reset the electrical.

We are laughing. Take as long as you want.

We arrive on the ground floor 28 minutes later. The doors open to a group of people waiting to get on the elevator. I look over at you and smile. You gently reach over and wipe a few drops of cum off my face.

We hold hands as we walk away wondering if the people getting on the elevator know what just happened in there.

*I*T'S EARLY MORNING; **I**'VE SNUCK INTO YOUR BEDROOM. **I** CRAWL up on your bed and place a very light feather kiss on your lips. You smile, like you expected me all along.

"Shhhh," I whisper.

Don't wake. Don't open your eyes. Don't move. Just feel.

I delicately place my lips on your neck, placing kisses along the base, working my way down your chest. My tongue brushes a nipple. You sigh, close to a moan.

Shhhh…just feel, receive, relax…let me adulate your naked body.

You groan softly.

I run the soft skin of my cheek along your chest like a kiss.

My fingertips glide along your neck and chest, the places my lips and tongue have been. So soft, touching so lightly it's difficult to feel, but I know you feel it.

I can tell. Your cock awakens a bit.

You are lying naked, half asleep on smooth navy blue sheets. You look like a Greek god.

I continue down your chest with the softest of kisses on your belly, low on your torso, just above your dark blond sex hair. Along the hairline…and your cock lets me know it's awake.

You moan, low and sleepily.

I skip over to your thighs…you sigh.

I continue to bathe you in light, barely discernable kisses and give just a small bite high on the inside of your thigh.

You moan a little louder.

Shhhh lover, stay in that dream place.

I continue down your legs slowly, deliberately, softly light kisses so light they are hard to discern, but you feel them. I feel the heat in your body grow.

Shhhhh

Don't open your eyes. Don't think. Don't speak. Stay in a dream-land.

Shhhhh

Later in the day you will wonder. "Was it real or did I dream it?"

I continue slowly…deliberately…softly.

The heat between us increases.

I can't wait any longer.

I breathe heavily on your cock. It's hard and my breath is invitation enough: it rises to meet my lips.

Shhhhh, don't wake yet.

Let me, this morning, be part of your morning.

You're hard in my mouth.

The thrill of you never ceases,

Shhhh

When you wake, smile!

BLAZE

I WANT ALL OF YOU TO FILL ME UP.
But go slow, you devil.

Make me beg for it.

"Please…please, I need you!"

I need you to fill me.

Fuck me.

Fuck me hard!

I want to feel your balls crash against me.

I want you to fuck me so hard my body moves across the bed. Make me feel your cum in me.

Make me cum so hard that I'm in a place where there are no words, no thoughts, no time.

Everything has stopped, just you and me suspended in pleasure for this moment.

Make love to me.

I want this.

*H*AVE YOU EVER HAD SEX SO INTENSE THAT IT FELT LIKE A spiritual experience?

There is cumming, and then there is moving to another plane.

The connection is so strong you know eternity must exist, based on this moment. It must feel like this, pure bliss, white light and shared soul connection with another person. There is good sex and then there is outer-worldly sex, sex that borders on rapture.

*G*O LIE DOWN.

Stroke yourself until you are incredibly hard.

Imagine me on top.

Riding you dripping wet, while playing with myself, cumming on your cock.

Because if I could, that is what I would be doing right now.

*L*OVER, YOU ARE SO NAUGHTY. YOU ASK ABOUT THE WICKEDEST things. Today you wish to know my masturbation habits. Last week you wanted to know my thoughts on voyeurism and exhibitionism. Are you planning something?

Well, lover, here is a little story I think you might enjoy. And covers both topics.

I have a friend named Sky. I know it sounds like a stripper name, but it's her real name. I had the good fortune of having her as a dear and close friend when I needed guidance, if you want to call it that. I learned a lot about sex from my friend Sky.

Sky and I became very close the summer after I graduated from high school. Sky is free-spirited and was far more sophisticated than I was about men and sex. She had a healthy sexual appetite. Actually, she is the first woman I knew who had lovers, several of them. She also grew up in a very different family setting than mine. Her parents were flower children (hence the name) and they were nudists. Sky had a real need to be free and naked. She hated clothes. She felt they were restricting. So often that summer we would go swim naked in the ocean. There are few things as wonderful on a hot summer night.

One night we went on a double date to the beach. We built a bonfire, roasted marshmallows, etc. Our dates didn't want to go in the water, so we did, naked. They never knew; boy, did they miss an opportunity.

We did a lot of crazy silly things, like many do at that age.

One day while driving...I drove a convertible at the time...we came upon a high-rise construction site, 20 floors up or so, not so high, but not low either. The workers on the top started with the catcalls.

Sky, ever the free spirit, pulled up her skirt and gave them all a nice look from a distance of her bush.

We laughed, and they went nuts.

We drove away.

We drove around the block, and they noticed the car and started to shout, "Let's see it all."

So I flashed them as well.

We drove around the block again. The workers noticed and went crazy.

Sky told me to pull into the parking lot across the street from the construction site. I did.

The guys up top noticed and were shouting at us.

Sky looked at me and said,

"I think this will be good for you, follow my lead."

She dropped the seat back to flat, put her fingers to her lips to make the signal for "shhhhh," and looked up at the guys, pulled up her skirt, pulled off her top, and started to finger herself for them.

They did quiet down, but they all looked, and the group became bigger.

She looked at me and said,

"You're not going to let me do this all alone? Are you?"

So I dropped the seat back, pulled up my skirt, and we masturbated for a group of 20 guys, 20 floors above us.

We both came, and then waved to the guys.

They kept mostly quiet until we were done. As we drove off they all shouted how much they loved us.

I had never masturbated in front of anyone, ever. I still remember how exhilarating the experience was.

Sky was a true free spirit and lover of sex.

I really can't believe I did something like that.

But I have come many times thinking about it.

I **HAD AN EROTIC DREAM.**
It was good.

You were in it.

*T*HE SCENE IS VERY DARK, LIT ONLY BY THOUSANDS OF WHITE TEA candles. Behind the first bar, floor to ceiling, is an altar of golden Buddhas. Two hallways lead devotees to the central bar and dance floor. Placed throughout the club are small pagodas of scantily clad women in Zen-like trances, in motionless yoga stances. This club is beyond hip, a cross between Buddhist temple and high-end bordello. You enter to worship in the city of sin. The line below is long. Entry for worship is gained one of three ways. Be in the know, have some dough, or wait.

I'm at the first bar, the place you start before delving deeper into the inner sanctums. I order three house specialties, unsure of what is in these libations.

Behind me, the elevator doors open. Exiting is a group of men all in suits, conventioneers who have gained entry by shelling out the bucks. Should have spent some money on hipper club attire, I think to myself.

I turn back to attend to the cocktails.

I pick up two drinks handing each to my fellow worshippers.

I pick up mine and turn. You are standing directly in front of me. Staring at me. Waiting for me to notice.

It takes me a moment to comprehend, such a surprise encounter. It's all out of context.

Introductions ensue, the suits to my friends, my friends to the suits.

Did you know I would be in Vegas?

Why are you in Vegas?

Basic logistical questions quickly move to more interesting conversations for everyone.

We all move toward the inner sanctums.

The music is very loud and primal.

The dance floor is jammed, packed with worshippers performing their rituals of celebration, intoxication, and vertical fornication.

In this club no one really cares what you do, short of violence.

You are leaning against the wall looking over the dance floor. At first, I'm next to you. We try to talk, but it is just too loud.

The constant ebb and flow of bodies moving to the rhythm pushes me directly in front of you. You pull me in close to keep people from passing through the space between us, until I am leaning up against you.

No words are spoken. We just watch the display of liturgy in this shrine to pleasure.

You place your hands low on my hips, slowly working down my pelvis, on the border of being indecent if anyone in this place cared about such things.

My hips are moving to the music. I can feel your cock harden against my ass. I like this feeling. It excites me. I feel warmth build in my lower chakras.

Your breath and then your mouth brush the base of my neck, which excites me even more. You are saying things into my ear, but

I can't hear the words, it's too loud, but I know what they mean. And I continue to move myself against you.

The song changes, to something impossible to resist; everyone must dance. We get pushed onto the dance floor. It is crowded and hot. The music is not fast or slow, but sensual and rhythmic... the type of music that makes people groin-grind each other in simulated sex and call it dancing.

I like the feeling of your hardness rubbing up against my thigh. And you know the effect it has on me. It fuels my desire. You can see it on my face.

Normally, I would feel uncomfortable with such a display in public, but this place and the rum (or was it tequila?) makes me feel sexy and uninhibited. With your body pressed up against mine, I'm in a pleasure trance.

We continue along with the crowd on the dance floor. You have one hand low on my back and move the other to the front. You like to keep your hands in front, don't you? Smart man!

You glide your fingers up under my skirt. It's short and not difficult to slip under. Sneaking your fingers under the elastic at the side of my panties...

You know where you're headed.

I've had enough rum or tequila, or whatever it was, to think no one can see, and if they can, I don't care.

Lightly you circle my clit with your finger. You know what you're doing. I think you enjoy pleasing women. I'm enjoying it right now.

We're still dancing, sort of, except you're making me cum with your fingers inside me.

Have you ever made a woman cum on a crowded dance floor? Was this a first?

My legs feel weak, my head falls back, and my body shudders involuntarily. I let out a low moan-gasp. If anyone could hear, they would understand the sound.

You have a satisfied smile on your face.

One orgasm, particularly the first, always makes me long to have another one.

And whether it was the rum, or maybe tequila, the sex daze, the music, or your body pressed against mine, I want you now, on this dance floor.

But the music changes and the dance floor thins, and despite the tequila (or was it rum?), I know it's just too much to attempt.

Moving to a chair in the back corner of the club, you sit. I straddle you, my skirt barely covering the top of my thighs; we make out. God, I love making out. Kissing, good kissing, is so sexy and fun. I don't know how anyone can do it for hours and not have sex. Possibly, I lack control.

You know what I want; thankfully you don't make me beg. You unzip and then pull my panties aside; a few people might have noticed, but they don't care. I put you inside me: Nirvana! You're so hard. You feel so unbelievably good inside me. Impossible to even try to speak. I'm in a place where there are no words. It's animal lust and paradise.

144

The deep desire to be filled, when met can be as quenching and satisfying as water after dehydration.

I rotate myself up and back and down on you, at first timidly to hide the obvious, and than less so. Let them watch. They can see nothing, but our movement gives us away. You like the audience.

Your hands are now under my skirt again. Yes, you definitely know where to go. Our private dance continues; our eyes are locked on each other. We both like to watch, and we know others are watching us. It's definitely the rum. I don't care if they watch, I'm watching you; I like to watch your face, your eyes, for the look of pleasure as you cum.

Do you want to dance?

I WANT MULTIPLE SEXUAL SLAVES AND A MAID.

*W*ERE YOU WAITING FOR ME?

Are you sitting in front of your computer?

Lean back in your chair, unzip, and take out your cock.

Do It!

Caress yourself.

Feels so good, it's flesh velvet.

Are you hard?

If not, we need to do something about that.

Hold your balls with your other hand and stroke yourself until you are hard.

Do It!

Now close your eyes and continue.

I'll be there with you.

Imagine me sucking you in deep; push my head down until my lower lip collides with the top of your balls.

You know how much I love it—hard between my lips.

I would stop…for a few tiny seconds of pleasure torture, but you tell me how good it feels and I don't have the heart to suspend your pleasure, even for a minute.

Your verbal encouragement makes me go at it harder. You tell me it's perfect…how could I possibly stop, with such praise?

Kneeling in front, you pull my hair up…are you watching?

I moan. It's not a conscious sound, simply an audible expression of desire and sex. I love sucking you.

You know this; can you tell even with your cock in my mouth that I'm smiling?

I pull you in deep.

Just enjoy, let me distract you for a few minutes.

I get so wet with you in my mouth. I've never cum while sucking cock, but you get me close.

You move with my mouth.

Go ahead, let me have your cum. If I could talk, this is what I would tell you.

Fuck my mouth.

Pull me down harder on you; I'll take you in.

That's it, cum! God you feel good!

You gonna come in my mouth?

On my tits?

Someplace else?

Wish I were there to lick cum dew off your fingers and the tip. Hmmmm.

Tell me about it after you cum.

I'M NERVOUS…OR IS IT EXCITED?

Possibly a bit scared, but still excited.

I could have said no, I could have …but somehow I can't.

I can never say no to you. Not ever.

When you call, I must answer.

You summon me, and I go.

I could resist, but I simply don't want to.

I like the way you make me feel.

I feel vulnerable around you. Of course, I would never let you know; I have too much pride to let you know you are my kryptonite.

But this request is different.

You are taking me into unknown territory.

A place I never thought I would visit…but it's you, I cannot say no.

Our encounters are always hot and, at times, manic.

Do we think the magic will dissipate if we move too slowly?

It is deep, our sexual connection.

No one has made me feel quite like you; that gives you power over me.

This alarms and excites me.

We connect in sex. I feel it, and I know you do too. We don't have to talk about it, it just is.

But this is different.

You want me to share you.

I have always known that I share you with others.

I don't think about it because I don't like to feel the jealousy of possessiveness.

We do not belong to each other, in traditional terms.

But when we are together, we are together!

The connection is solid.

I'm insecure. I'm not worldly enough and too naïve.

I'm the third wheel.

I don't like to share, not in sex. I want you to myself.

But sharing is what you want of me and I cannot say no, not to you.

Everything is friendly and nice. Your girlfriend is lovely. I like her instantly. I feel no animosity toward her, just pangs of envy. She has daily what I only have for scattered brief moments.

I know why I'm here. But I need more courage. Drinks…ah yes, I'm sure that will help. You both smoke a bit of pot. I confess that I have never smoked…anything.

Your girlfriend moves, and before I know what has happened she has pushed her mouth against mine and shared her hit with me. Her lips linger on mine. I feel paralyzed. Her tongue circles my lips slowly. Still, I can't seem to move. I'm frozen.

In time, I pull away.

I need to begin with what I know, before I can jump into the unknown. I need you to initiate. And you do.

You command me to kiss you. I'm thrilled. I love kissing you. It was your unbelievable talent for kissing that got me to this place. You kiss me, and the world fades. Only our pleasure exists. That first time was one of the most erotic moments of my life. Kissing evolved to making out, petting, and then some.

It was scintillating.

When you moved your fingers, wet from being deep inside me, and put them in your mouth to taste my flavor, I watched in amazement as you told me how good I tasted. And how much you would enjoy making me cum using your tongue. It was one of the most erotic things I had ever seen a man do.

I knew then, we would be lovers.

But now I'm kissing you with your girlfriend watching. I always thought I would enjoy an audience, but I feel intimidated and shy. I comment on her watching, and she assures me it's fine. She likes to watch you with others, she says. I move away. I'm going to have to ease into this scenario. The idea of an audience is exciting, but I always imagined them as anonymous.

I want you so desperately. We try again. A group kiss, all three tongues and mouths. It really has no sexual effect on me except while kissing I take the opportunity to rub your cock. Now, this I like. I always want your cock. It's so beautiful, and you are hard. You like knowing two women are there for you.

I feel like an awkward virgin, not knowing how to play this new game. You assure me that we'll only go as far as I feel comfortable. I lie back on the rug. The alcohol has produced the desired effect.

You move down and kiss me. Ah yes, this I know, this I like. Kissing you is persuasive. You move on top of me; I love the heaviness of your body on me, slowly pushing yourself into my sex. You are weakening my apprehensions.

She watches us and I begin to enjoy her presence. She offers gentle encouragement. You whisper, "She really wants to watch you blow me."

I love to suck your dick. You know this.

This is my one true weakness, my one true fetish.

I suspect you both had a plan to seduce me with what I love and then introduce me into the unknown.

I crave your cock in my mouth. So I take the invitation.

You roll to your back. Still kissing, I slide my hand down, unbuckle your belt, and unzip your jeans.

The feeling of you hard is incredible. I love the combination of hard with the delicate soft skin. I can't wait to place my lips over the tip and slide down until you are in deep. With my nose resting against your pubic hair, I take in your scent.

It's like the beginning of a concert or the first run of the day when skiing, the rush of the initial pleasure of you in my mouth is forever present, no matter how many times before.

I lick the tip, slide down the shaft and back up again, before I take all of you in. You are watching. You always like to watch. She is watching as well. I suddenly feel the rush of performing not only for you, but also for her.

I smile and start the show.

Time passes, and I bring you close and then back away. You don't get to cum yet. This is my show.

She moves over to us, unbuttons your shirt, and begins to kiss you. Starting at your lips, she works her way down your chin and neck, biting your nipples, and continues to move down your stomach to the edge of your sex hair. Your sounds of pleasure confirm what your body is telling us. You adore being served by two women.

I move to the side, and she begins to lick your shaft while I work the tip …moving our lips and tongues up and down until we are both sharing your cock like a lollypop. I look up at you. Your eyes are closed and your lips are in a sly smile.

She gently pulls my head in towards her, until our lips touch with your cock in the middle. I focus on your cock, and she is concentrating on kissing me. The oddness of this strikes me, I am licking you and kissing her at the same time. Our mouths have made a sandwich around your cock. I know you like this, being the center of our sexual Oreo.

In time, she moves away; I have your cock all to myself, and I cherish not having to share.

She moves her mouth back up your body until she reaches your mouth and then laughingly states, "Oh you're not going to be the one to have all the fun."

Still laughing, she removes her jeans and straddles your face.

I envy her boldness.

I envy the orgasm she definitely will have, knowing how talented you are with your tongue. I envy the uninhibited way she screams and moans while grinding herself onto your face... not knowing if this is normal or amplified for my benefit.

Inspired by her bold lead, I leave the safety of sucking you and move up to enjoy how hard we've made you.

I push my skirt up, pull my thong to the side, and glide you into me. You are so hard, and I'm so wet. Again, always, the initial sensation of your cock entering me is exhilarating.

You have too much to concentrate on to be of much help, but that is okay...I don't need you to do anything except stay hard. I will do the rest. I start slow, raising myself up almost until you leave me and then down, my intensity and speed increasing as my excitement builds.

Your girlfriend notices I have taken liberties to ride you as well. She leans back and orders me to kiss her.

Why not?

I know you are watching. I do it for you, always…anything for you.

I lower my lips to her and proceed to kiss her as if I were kissing you. For a few minutes, for your voyeuristic pleasure, we kiss. Gently biting each other's lips, tongues dancing in and out of each other mouths. It's soft, sensual, and very erotic. We both know this performance is for you.

I know you enjoyed our show. I feel you grow even harder in me. I take this as encouragement and pull away from her lips, and I now focus on pushing myself down deeper onto you. Forcefully pistoning my hips up and down on you. I might have been slow to warm to this game, but I'm all in now.

Your girlfriend saddles up behind me and begins to kiss my neck. Did you tell her? You know this makes me crazy. I lean back, allowing you to watch your cock slide in and out.

She reaches around and begins to finger my clit as I fuck you. For a brief moment I stop, thinking, is this too much?

I resolve not to think. It's easier to just feel.

I always think too much.

I'm close. I feel my body on the edge. Her fingers circle my clit like it's hers. You like watching this as well, I know. You like your two blondes having sex while having sex with you.

I start to come, so hard my body shakes, my back aches, my head rolls back, mouth open, gasping for more air, while pressing myself deep onto you. I continue to crash into you, knowing you were just waiting for me. I feel you, I know you are coming, she knows you are coming, and with her other hand she reaches back and squeezes the cum from your balls. You moan deeply, and I feel all of you in me. It's marvelous. It's always amazing with you.

Everything begins to slow down; I fall forward and kiss you. I start to laugh. We all laugh. "Only for you, lover, only for you." I whisper.

You whisper in my ear, "She wants to taste you. I told her how good you taste. Let her lick my cum from you."

I laugh, nervously. Wow! I'm not sure I'm ready for all of that.

I'm thinking too much again. I roll off of you.

You know I'm stalling. You roll over to kiss me; she is on the other side of you.

"How about if we share you?"

You are convincing, and she is smiling. Reaching over to stroke my cunny as you try to sell me on the idea.

You know how to tempt a girl. Just thinking about your tongue on me anytime, anywhere, excites me.

You are truly talented, having a gift for oral pleasure.

Past girlfriends must have had trouble ever leaving you, for that single reason alone. A few drinks and I would be calling like a cat in heat.

I never call you. I wish I could. But I know that is not our relationship. You call, and I never say no.

You have a gift for sex. And now that I've been given it, average fucking will never satisfy, ever again.

I know you both think you are going to get your way.

You finger me, while convincing me with your kisses. She is pressed up behind you, caressing you and then me. Once again, you are a sandwich, but this time between our bodies.

I close my eyes and enjoy your fingers getting me off. Your lips are on me, my neck, ah, now you are cheating. You know this makes me crazy.

She is stroking you from behind. You are hard again. I feel you press into my thigh. Your cock against me, I love it. You are playing dirty, trying to get what you want.

You pull your wet fingers from me, move them towards your mouth, and then reach back and feed them to her. She licks each finger like it's your cock.

She wants to suck your cum out of me, I hear her say, as you feed her your dewy fingers one by one.

This excites and scares me at the same time.

You know this about me without me having to say a word. In sex we connect. Our understanding is absolute.

I think, "Do what you know. Do what you love."

I roll you on your back clasp my mouth around your cock. This time I'm in charge. You are going to cum. And fast. I'm relentless. My mouth, my tongue, and both hands have a mission: you are going to come, and come NOW!

I call it the ultra blow. And it works. You can't help but come. I catch all of you in my mouth and pull off just as you finish. I grab your girlfriend by the hair and pull her lips to me and share all of your taste, with her inches from your face. She sucks all of your cum from my mouth. We lean over and kiss you, three mouths and three tongues.

I begin to make my exit before you can work your spell on me again. I'm feeling a bit like Alice in Wonderland. I have fallen down the rabbit hole.

*T*HERE ARE TIMES WHEN LOVE NEEDS NO WORDS, ONLY ACTION.

"*H*AVE YOU EVER THOUGHT ABOUT BEING WATCHED?" Your entire message.

I respond,

"What are you proposing?"

Your answer,

"I have a friend who likes to watch."

Me, "Just watch?"

You, "Yes."

Me, "This friend male or female?"

You, "Male."

My response,

"I think there is more to this story."

Your response,

"What do you mean?"

Me, "A male friend who likes to watch? How does that come up in casual conversation?"

Me, after a pause, "I suspect he likes to watch you. I can't really blame him. I enjoy watching you as well."

You respond, "Could be. He watched me about 10 years ago and enjoyed it. Think it over. He's up for it if you are."

I respond, "Does this excite you?"

You, "It does."

Me, "I'm intrigued for sure. It's sexy, it's different, and it excites you."

Exciting you is what I like best.

Me, "I'm shy."

You, "I'm shy too. But we only live once and it will be fun. Let me know."

Me, "Nous vivons seulement une fois."

You, "What does that mean?"

Me, "We only live once."

You, "YES!"

Me, "Oui."

You, "Merci."

Me, "De nada."

*L*IGHT KNOCK.

Me, "You came alone?"

Your response, "He's in the bar. He'll be up in a few."

This ends our conversation. I push you up against the wall, my mouth attacking your lips.

I'm so aggressive. I'm nervous. I'm overcompensating.

Mental note of how nice you look as I run my hands across your white dress shirt. I wonder, are you extra spiffy for me or for him?

I still think there's more to the story between you two, but right now I don't care. My body wants as much of you as I can have.

Undressing you while my fingers and mouth devour your flesh. You help.

I think you want to be naked before your friend arrives. I notice the cuff links, very nice. Definitely fancier today; is this for me? Or for him? Both?

You're naked lying on the bed, my body between your legs, my face nestled at your cock. I look up…you're watching.

Grinning, I ask "So what do you want?"

Followed by "May I?"

I don't wait for a response as I let my tongue take in the first taste, collecting a little dew from the tip. My lips glide down your shaft. I know you like it. I can hear your approval.

In a cock-induced trance, I don't hear the knock, but you do.

You were waiting for the knock. There is more to this story, I know it.

I answer the door, quick greetings to the stranger/friend who is now our audience.

"There's beer in the fridge." I say as I rush back.

Like a Greek god, you're reclined naked across the bed. My eyes take in your body; I adore a naked man.

There is more to this story.

I return your cock to my mouth. It calms me, like a pacifier.

I'm nervous.

Am I excited? Not sure. The current scenario hasn't yet sunk in.

Our audience moves quietly about and you ask me quietly if "I'll suck him too?"

I knew it. I knew it!

I knew there was going to be a soft sell for a threesome. I ask if this would excite you.

You say, "yes."

Now more insistent on getting me undressed, you are pulling at my clothes until my blouse, bra, skirt, and panties are flung about the room. This stranger friend can see my bare ass as I suck you.

I suck you like it's my life force.

I am nervous.

I glance quickly at our audience. He is sitting naked and stroking himself. I'm not sure what I expected to see, but this surprised me. When did he get undressed?

Knowing he was naked helped calm me. Feels like we are all in this together, not just performing for him.

I relax, a little.

You flip me over and finally enter me.

You like fucking me.

Your words confirmed it. I actually don't know what you said, but I heard, "Now that's what I'm talking about!" and feel you push harder into me. Kneeling, chest up, you face our audience of one. On my back, I am unable to see if he is looking at you or me. I ask him, our stranger friend, who he's watching and he answers "Both of you."

I know there is more to this story.

You in me…sexual bliss. Not caring who is watching. Just fuck me please, don't stop.

You ask where you should come.

You know my answer is "anywhere you want."

I think you are showing off for your friend. I am open to what will please you. I barely answer.

And you moan "tits" as you pull out and shoot across my chest.

Our audience is very quiet, but I sneak a peek at him stroking himself.

I notice he has a tattoo next to his groin. I do not look close enough to discern the image. Besides, I now have you back in my mouth as I suck you into my submission once again.

I want to ask our audience questions, but I'm unsure about what role I should play in this new game. A game I think you both have played before. I want to know if he's sucked a cock. Does he want to suck this cock? Has he? Would you let him?

My mouth is busy. I ask none of my questions, but my mind continues to wonder.

You need a few moments to recover; I crawl up and straddle you. I rub my pussy across your cock as you finger me. It feels so good I don't care that he is watching.

I ask him what he would like to see, and his answer is he is enjoying everything so far.

You ask me if I'm close. I answer "yes."

"You do it and let us watch." you whisper.

I'm panicked.

Masturbating in front of my lover is intimate. I've done it before but I felt very exposed. Now I'm performing for two. I close my mind to the anxiety, look straight into your eyes and finger myself. Grinding my pelvis into yours, leaning back onto one arm, arching my back so you can see me, see my lips open, glossy and excited. I continue to watch you watch me. Wondering if my getting myself off is exciting to your friend. I hold nothing back: I expose everything. I come hard. The room smells of my pussy. I collapse on you.

Back to your cock, I take you in my mouth. You are hard again.

You roll me over; you like fucking me from the back. I like you fucking me.

As you enter, you say something about my sweet ass and glide your hands over it and push yourself in even deeper. No words for how good you feel. I can only moan a sound that is deep and primal. I stretch my arms out and look up, expecting to see our audience, but he has now moved. He's sitting behind you.

I think there is more to this story.

I reach back with one hand to stroke your balls; you are hard, I can feel you are close. I wonder if your friend wishes to touch you, move in behind you? Maybe he is fingering your ass as you fuck me. I cannot see him. Anything is possible.

You don't ask, this time as you shoot your cum across my ass.

You fall on your back and I return to what I love…sucking your cock. You laugh.

"There's no way."

But I don't give up so easy. With you deep in my mouth, you ask again "If I would suck him."

Somehow I knew the question would come up again. "Would this excite you?" I ask.

"Yes." you whisper.

Wanting to excite you, I move over to our audience. Moving from the bed to his chair without asking permission or even looking at him I put his cock in my mouth.

He's shaved, something I didn't notice until now.

I say something about not promising to finish the job but if this will excite you I will suck him a bit.

He moves to the bed, I return to his cock, and you move behind me. I can't see you now. You rest your hands on my ass. Are you watching him or me?

Say something. Let me know this is exciting to you.

The stranger reaches down to my breasts and pinches my nipples. He pulls away and I roll over looking for you.

"See, he doesn't like it."

"Oh yes he does!" you exclaim.

He came, but I didn't even notice. But you knew he came, you had a towel ready for him. Was he watching you as he came?

I think there is more to this story.

THE BIG APPLE! A CITY LIKE NO OTHER! THE BUZZ OF HUMAN electricity is everywhere. A place you can be alone if you choose, while surrounded by a community of millions.

I'm waiting for you.

Your text reads, "Running late."

I message back. "How late?"

No response.

I'm at The Monkey Bar, a good place for monkey business, a retro hip bar attached to my hotel.

The bar becomes quite the scene much later in the night. But now the place is mostly empty, except for a couple making out in a red leather booth in the back.

I'm sitting at the bar, drinking a Manhattan. When in Rome…! It's a very adult and lethal cocktail.

An affluent looking man in his late 40's sits next to me. Sunglasses on indoors, five cell phones he lays on the bar, and four huge shopping bags from Bergdorf's.

My guess is he has many women, maybe even wives, and this is how he keeps them all straight. Maybe it's the years I spent behind the bar, but I enjoy getting the back-story on strangers; often it's good entertainment.

Cell phone man confesses he is a private investigator. I don't believe him, but it's his story so I let him tell it. I'm just passing time. He shows me all of his purchases; now I'm really convinced he has many women. He asks why I'm sitting at the bar alone. I tell him I'm waiting for a friend. He raises one eyebrow with a quizzical look. I know what he is concluding; I let on nothing, let him wonder.

One of the phones buzzes and he promptly leaves.

Next, three older ladies come in, sit at the bar, tourists from Florida, but they let me know they used to live on the upper Eastside. They have just come back from a big day of shopping. Their acquisitions have made them giddy, along with the gin, and they tell me all about the best shops in Manhattan. People in New York can be very friendly when it suits them. I'm moving into my second Manhattan and wonder how late you're going to be.

Next, two girls I place in their 20's come in dressed in club attire. Is it that late? Are the hipsters starting to arrive already? They sit next to me at the bar as if I were waiting for them. They include me in their conversation and eventually ask what I'm doing by myself. These girls act as if we have been friends for years. I'm tipsy, waiting and willing to join in their fun. This is their first stop before heading to Midtown. I tell them my situation without any names. They enjoy my story.

They tell me to message you and let you know you are too late. I have new friends now. I pretend to send the message to you.

The music starts as I start in on my third Manhattan, which I know is too many.

Where the hell are you?

I suspect you are not coming.

These girls, dancers by profession, are up the second the music starts. And as their newest friend, I am encouraged to dance. I've never been afraid of a dance floor, and as the music continues, their dancing becomes more suggestive. I play along. I used to do the same thing many years ago to attract attention. Nothing like two women (or now, three) sauntering up to each other to the rhythm in order to get others to notice. Their dancing becomes more erotic, outsiders try to enter our group, but my new friends want nothing to do with these trespassers. I'm sweaty from dancing with these two sexy 20-somethings. Their dance moves are becoming more suggestive. We are in a three-way hip roll when I look up and see you watching. You are smiling, that all-knowing smile. The smile that makes me think you know exactly what I'm thinking. The smile knows I want you. I walk straight to you and plant my lips on yours pressing all of my body into yours. I want no space between us. I want every part of your body to feel every part of my desire.

My new friends have followed me to you. When I break away from you, the taller girl pulls me back to her and plants her lips on mine with all the intensity I just gave you. Surprised, and too tipsy to react quickly, I sway as she lets me go while the shorter one says it's her turn and pulls me forward to her lips.

Knowing you are watching, I kiss her. I kiss her as if I'm kissing you. Our mouths open, lips parted, and tongues moving in exploration. The taller girl moves in from behind and begins to rub my tits. She places her lips on my neck, all the while looking at you. She knows you're watching. She knows you like the show.

I pull away, grab you by the hand and pull you to the bar. You need a drink. I need to level the playing field. Our new friends pull up beside us.

They give you a good amount of shit for making me wait so long. I laugh. You take it in stride. Without any verbal foreplay the taller of the girls announces she wants to watch us fuck.

I laugh at her boldness, and, maybe because of the third Manhattan, without thinking I tell her I want to watch them first. Without even a second of hesitation they say yes.

I glance at you. You're smiling. You've set me up.

You profess you didn't. But I know this is a dream come true for you. You are smiling.

I whisper, "You're a lucky man, you are."

Up to my room we go. In the elevator the girls make out. Not one to just watch, I lean back into you, letting my ass feel your cock, which is hard from their show.

In the room the girls continue to make out, clothing flying off as they pounce on the closest bed.

We lie on the other bed watching their show, while your hands move up under my blouse to my nipples.

You kiss my neck as we watch these young beautiful strangers make love. Enjoying each other thoroughly. Doubting they remember we are there.

I'm not one to just watch. I've waited too long for you to arrive. I move my body to face you. We start our own show.

Clothes on, I move myself on top of you. I grind my cunt against your cock while removing your tie and then your shirt, until the top half of you is naked.

Moving down, I unfasten your belt, unzip your slacks, and discard it all to the floor.

Finally naked, I look at you smiling and watching. You know what is next.

I look at you and ask, "What do you want?"

You smile.

I know the answer.

The girls now watch us. You like this very much, I know.

They say I make cock-sucking look so good they want to try it.

Reluctantly, I move away letting them have you. I know this is a dream come true for you, but I don't like sharing.

They take turns. I watch.

The taller one then boldly straddles your face and tells you to eat her. I admire her boldness. Oh, I know you like this.

Her girlfriend, intrigued, moves up to kiss her friend. Facing each other and straddling your face, they make out and grind their sexes together.

I briefly worry you can't breathe, but then I see you slide your hands up the legs of the girls. You love this.

I move back to what I love, your cock in my mouth.

You are very hard; no one is paying the least bit of attention to what I'm doing, so I slide myself onto your cock.

I ride you slowly. I'm working on my own enjoyment. You are more than busy at the moment. I suspect your tongue is working its circular magic on each of their clits.

Pleasing three women at once; I know if your mouth and tongue were not so busy you would be smiling.

I close my eyes and let my body feel you hard in me.

I open my eyes, and our new friends are now watching me ride your cock. You are smiling, your face shiny from the dew of our young friends.

The taller one moves up behind me and begins to circle my clit while the smaller one coaxes my nipples into hard nubs.

I know you are watching.

I let my head drop back and she understands. Her lips move to mine. And our tongues intertwine while you watch. I know you like the show. I can feel it. You are hard and getting harder as I slide up and down you glistening cock. The tension builds until my body spasms in blissful release.

I still think you set me up. But at this moment, I don't mind.

I see your Cheshire cat grin as you watch me cum.

I love NYC.

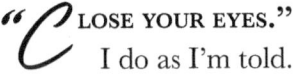 **LOSE YOUR EYES."**
I do as I'm told.

I feel the cool silkiness of the material as it brushes along my face. You tighten the satin over my eyes and knot it.

"A blindfold, should be fun," I murmur.

You walk me along, careful to guide me.

Ours steps creak on the wooden floor. It is true, take away the sense of sight and the other senses become suddenly sharper. You lead me left onto carpet, which feels lush under my bare feet.

You direct me to sit. It's a large chair, very plush. Music is playing, worldly foreign mystical rhythms with a strange sexy sound.

You take my hands and rest them on the chair's arms, and suddenly I hear "click click."

You've handcuffed me.

I laugh and then stop.

Feeling my anxiety, you whisper close to my ear "Nothing, my sweet, will happen that you won't enjoy."

I relax a little. I relax more when I feel your lips on mine.

It's a peculiar feeling being kissed but not being able to see when it's coming.

Your lips move down my neck; you know my weakness. I feel myself melting into submission.

You unbutton my blouse. Placing gentle kisses on the top of my breasts.

I become more aware of the music…did it get louder?

You remove my skirt, leaving my panties on.

You tongue me though the sheer fabric.

Yes! I'm excited…I can smell my desire in the room already.

You stroke my legs…and then nothing.

Did you leave? I ask if you are there. I hear only the music.

Then I feel two hands, massaging my upper shoulders. Are these your hands? They seem softer and smaller.

I feel silken cloth against my chest. It tickles.

It brushes up my chest to my face and then I feel the pull as the silk presses between my lips.

Blindfolded, handcuffed, and now gagged, my anxiety level again rises.

You sense this again and whisper in my ear, "Nothing, my sweet will happen that you will not enjoy."

You pacify me again with kisses at the base of my neck and soothe me like a frightened child.

As you do this I feel that cool silky cloth again along my thighs.

Someone else is here!

You whisper reassurances as the cloth tightens around my ankles, first the left then the right.

I sense warm breath on my legs. Then the warm breath is just above my panties.

I feel the hands stroking on my legs as I am being tongued through my panties.

You coo in my ear. "Enjoy...let yourself go...don't worry... relax... let yourself feel wonderful."

You persuade me with words and kisses along my neck. I feel the welcoming sensations of lust and desire replacing my fear and anxiety.

Just as I begin to enjoy the attention, a hard, cold object placed against my skin jolts me. It's resting against my belly, and I feel it glide down under my panties. It's cold metal headed to my...then I hear the sound.

'Snip snip snip' and my panties are cut away. One firm pull and the strip of fabric is gone.

I am naked except for my bra and my blouse, which is behind my back with the sleeves pulled down to my elbows, further restricting my movement.

You whisper, "enjoy, my sweet," as you continue to caress me.

The mouth returns to my now naked pussy.

This tongue knows how to please. It licks and flicks my clit. Then, with gentle circles, it hones in on my pleasure spots.

You are watching all this. I cannot see you, but I know you are watching. You like watching. I finally let go; I cum in rhythmic spasms until I've soaked the chair.

You continue your whispers in my ear, "Do you know how exciting your body is to watch?"

I can say nothing; I can do nothing. I am left in a position of complete submission. I can only accept...a place I've never been before.

"Accept and enjoy," you murmur in my ear.

Hands. New hands? I think so, but I can't tell.

Oh yes, new mouth on my pussy. The style is different.

You continue your whisperings while stroking my breasts.

My nipples become erect and taut.

The mouth leaves and I feel…oh yes, a stiff cock.

It's not yours because you are beside me.

You are watching as this cock enters my slick pussy.

Unable to move, I accept this fucking as you stroke me.

You tell me to submit, love the feeling, accept the pleasure without giving anything back.

I cum again while the cock continues to fuck me.

Based on what I hear and feel, he came too.

I wonder how many mouths and cocks I will experience today in my captive condition.

Another mouth. Is it the same or a different mouth?

This mouth lovingly licks me clean of the remainders of the cock that drips from my pussy. I am learning to accept and enjoy.

I feel selfish.

Another cock enters me.

Ah… I know this cock.

I know it's you. You press your whole body into mine. I feel all of you in me, on me, but I cannot touch you. You push into me slow and hard. You whisper again and again "accept and enjoy" as you push farther and farther in.

Your rhythm is slow, rubbing against my swollen clit as if we were slow dancing. I feel you cum and it triggers yet another orgasm in me. You lean on me, and whisper how beautiful I look.

You ease yourself off me and I feel silky material drape across my body. I hear the music. I hear no one else. You remove my binds and kiss me.

I'M IN A MOOD!

I'm in a mood of aggressive randiness.

I want to push you down on the bed, hard.

Shove you on your back and attack.

If I had a way to tie you up, I would.

I'll find a way.

I want you as my captive.

I feel no gentle loving caresses at the moment.

I want raw sex.

I want to rip off your pants, and stick you in my mouth.

You'll lie there and take it.

I'm going to suck you until I'm satisfied.

Oh, don't think I'll let you cum. No. No. No!

I said I was going to suck you, until I'm satisfied.

I can tell when you're close. I'll stop just short. You are not cumming, not until I'm satisfied.

I want to suck on you until my mouth aches from stretching over your engorged cock.

The next day I want the skin on your cock to be sensitive from all the work I gave it the night before. Painful pleasure.

I told you I'm in a mood!

Oh, you'll enjoy it, but it will be a bit painful.

Sweet agony.

I'm going to suck every last bit of power out of your dick.

When I'm done, you'll need rest.

Having your cock in my mouth makes me feel powerful.

I'm going to suck you until you are steel and then impale myself on your cock.

I'm going to ride you until I cum all over your dick and balls. Fucking until I cum again and again.

I told you, I'm in a mood!

Wanton sex is what I need. And you are my victim.

And don't cum, not yet, not until I'm satisfied.

If you make the unfortunate mistake of cumming while I'm fucking you... well then I'm going to ride your face.

And you'll lie there and take it. Suffocating you with my wet pussy.

Oh, I'll rub myself across your face and mouth so hard you'll be wishing you had your dick to rescue you from my insatiable needs; ramming my clit against your tongue so hard you'll think it's sprained the next day.

This is sex we are going to feel for days!

I'm in a mood!

*L*IKE A SCENE FROM A MOVIE, WELL THE SEXY PART ANYWAY. No pre-planning no racy intentions…just walking home through the city and passing an old fancy hotel. I love the architecture of old buildings; the ceilings and walls were made to be beautiful, not just functional.

We consider a nightcap at the dark, wooden carved bar, but decide to keep exploring first. The black-and-white pictures on the walls display formal turn-of-the-century galas, visits from past dignitaries and celebrities. Our wandering takes us to the entrance of a banquet hall; I'm sure it is gilded and grand like the rest of the hotel, but sadly, the doors are locked. To the side is a service entrance: we check…not locked…and gain access this way to the hall.

It is gloriously ostentatious, as expected. Carved marble columns, golden glided walls, and dozens of magnificent crystal chandeliers.

In our adventuring through this wonderfully ostentatious hall, we discover that to the side of the large hall is an opening to a smaller banquet room. We, of course, enter this room to discover it is not as majestic as the main hall but still old-world splendid.

There is a piano in this parlor, and you sit down to play. I didn't even know you knew how to play…so many things I don't know about you. But I would like to find out more, if you would just let me.

We had sex before dinner. I can't help it. You gave me a window in which to play, and I took it. Best appetizer ever. I would rather have sex than eat, sleep, or pretty much anything I think you were not expecting me to take it as far as I did—but we got busy on the floor until at least *I* came, my favorite appetizer course done.

Post-dinner bliss in a magnificent old hotel with the man I love playing the piano for me in a hall that has hosted thousands of grand events for over a century…it is a scene from a movie.

I stand behind you as you play, pressing my body into your back; I run my hands down your chest as you continue to serenade. My hands want more and slide down to your cock; you are hard, and that's all the invitation I need.

I sit to your side on the piano bench, plant my lips on yours, and unzip your pants. Within seconds you are in my mouth. You are hard, really hard. It's like it was planned, but it wasn't. You, quietly, as to not disturb the silence of this grand room, let me know you are indeed enjoying this post-dinner nightcap. I want to straddle you and fuck you here…it seems too much to attempt, but I keep thinking it as I continue to suck your cock. Your cock in my mouth makes me so incredibly horny.

I am soaking wet, I want you to fuck me, I'm reconsidering the idea of fucking on the piano bench, but I know you, lover, I know your sounds and your body, you are close, and this excites me too. I take you in deep and you hold my head there, I breathe in the smell of your sex, your cock, your balls. You whisper, "I'm gonna cum. I'm gonna cum. I'm gonna cum. Oh my God, I'm cumming!"

You shoot down my throat, and we just stay in this place. You collapse your body over mine as I hold your cock still in my mouth. We stay folded together this way. I could stay this way all night. But the sex trance soon breaks, and we realize where we are. We are quiet as we re-dress. But we smile at each other.

I love when you cum. I'm a giver. I love making you feel good. I love how crazy exciting blowing you in this old hotel is to me. I wonder how much sex has happened in this banquet room. We are not the first, I'm sure…if only the walls could talk. We've added to the erotic history of this historic landmark. I love making history, don't you?

*L*ONG STROKES AS IF YOU WERE PAINTING A FENCE WITH YOUR tongue you lap up my essence. I moan, completely relaxed, as you focus on wiggling and working your tongue into my ass, darting your warm tongue in and out.

The feeling is narcotic, releasing endorphins into my body, erasing everything but pure carnal sensation.

My pussy lies open, dark pink lips extremely swollen…you look up, catching my eyes, and tell me I'm a masterpiece.

You tell me you have dreamt of falling asleep with your mouth on my pussy, suckling it like a baby.

*T*HE MESSAGE SAID, "BE THERE AT EIGHT. DON'T BE LATE. I HAVE a surprise."

Your messages are always short and detail lacking.

A "surprise." Hmmmm, I like that. You always surprise me. Every time it is a surprise. Every day you pull me into your excitement, living for the joys of each moment.

"Don't be late." Your voice was playful, but I know you mean it. I'm always late. I don't mean to be. I hate being late. Alas, life seems to be filled with constant distractions and time-sucking irritations.

You know I will spend all day thinking about the "surprise." I wonder if we are staying in or going out? What should I wear? Such a "girl" thing to think.

So much curiosity…a huge array of ideas go through my brain. "A surprise." What could it be? What could it be? I'm slightly giddy thinking about it.

I arrive at your place, five to eight. You answer the door. "I'm not late." I say playfully.

You smile and kiss me quickly on the lips to say 'hello.'

You take me by the hand and lead me down the hall to the bedroom. Ah, the surprise will be in your lair. Some of my favorite surprises have taken place here.

The room is glowing, candles everywhere. A delicious aroma fills the air from their flame, vanilla, cinnamon and sugar cookies? A warm and comforting scent that makes me want to lick the air.

You playfully push me on your bed. I love your bed, so inviting, as if it hugs you back when you lie on it.

You quickly undress, you know I like you best this way, naked. I love the feel of our skin touching, no clothes blocking the sensation, our warmth transferring back and forth, generating energy and the nuances of activities to come. You are hard already. I like that too. I give it a lick. You push me back flat on the bed.

You are directing this show and I willingly submit.

You slowly begin to undress me, applying attention, kisses, caresses, and love bites to every new area you uncover. I lie back and enjoy. You enjoy this…and I used to try to rush, but now I just savor you loving me slowly, inch by inch. The time and detail invested in exploring each part of my body makes me incredibly aroused.

So completely overcome with excitement, you make me come before we have even started the main event.

Selfishly, I lie back and accept as you lick your way up from my toes, to the inside of my knees, deep and high on the inside of my thighs, quickly you lightly brush over my clit, enough to make me moan for more, but then you move on. "Playful torture" you call it.

Before I grew to appreciate your torturous ways, I would ache, feeling physical pain from the lack of attention on my more erotic zones. Now, I know you will get there in your sweet time, savoring the built-up tension, which heightens all sensations. I know you'll circle back to my most sensitive areas. You'll lovingly lick me until I truly can't take it any more, and only then will you let me feel you hard inside me. I'm about to come just thinking about it.

My body now craves the meticulous attention of your lips, fingers, and tongue. My legs, lips, and body open to you, inviting you to enter. Welcoming your mouth as your tongue laps at my dark blushing lips, glossy from excitement.

I love the way you lick me. Sucking on my sex hairs, nibbling on my clit, fucking me with your tongue. You change speeds, rhythm, cadence, and intensity. You are a master. You love this. It is your drug. Happily, I supply your fix. The level of your excitement from just tonguing me is amazing. I know you have come from just going down on me. I do understand this; I love you hard in my mouth just as much. We are oral people…this we share.

Today, your tongue paints pleasure on my entire body, and I passively enjoy.

Sometimes I'm very active and aggressive, grinding myself into your tongue, pulling your head down on me, forcing my sex on your face, smothering you with my wetness.

You like it when I'm rough, it excites me as well, but today I am gentle. I let the waves of pleasure just sweep over my body. This is your party and your 'surprise,' so I lazily let you direct the action.

My excitement and level of desire grows with each orgasm. I always want more. I'm insatiable. You know this about me and you want me wanting.

Quietly you say, "Do you want to know the surprise?"

Surprise? I had forgotten. You had erased any cognitive thoughts from my mind. I was focused on pleasure, pure physical pleasure. All id.

Regaining the ability to speak in an understandable language, I answer, "Yes, of course."

In reality, I thought I had already enjoyed my 'surprise.'

As if on cue, there is a ring at the door.

You smile. "Surprise time."

Smiling at me with a face shiny from pleasing me, you throw on some lounge pants…still sporting an impressive hard on.

"I wish you would let me suck on that," I say as you walk towards the door.

You answer with a smile, and say,

"When you feel ready, there's a package under the bed; put it on and come out to join us."

Smiling, you leave our sex haven to get the door.

Now you have me thinking again, hmmm…

I lie naked in a catatonic dreamlike euphoria from your tongue bath. You love me so completely. You make my body scream your name and ache with desire when I can't have you.

My mind starts ticking away; my mind is almost always ticking. That is why you are so precious to me; only you can make my body's sensations override my nearly-never-quiet brain. You make it impossible for me to think. I can only feel. Oh god, your tongue circling my clit, lapping up my juice makes me dizzy with desire.

I feel myself get wetter with this thought.

"Surprise? Package? Join us?"

Lover what have you planned?

I hear you and another voice. The voice is male.

"What is the surprise?"

I reach under the bed. I find a large, fancy gift box, tied with a single shiny black satin bow.

I untie the ribbon and lift up the lid. Under the swanky tissue is an exquisite Chinese-style silk robe. The fabric is a vibrant red, sewn with gossamer gold thread. The robe is so soft yet the fabric has weight, which is deceiving since the garment is nearly see-through. I wrap it around me, so luxurious. I feel like a movie star. The red, the robe…all of it looks good on me. You know how to dress women.

I reach again into the box, pulling out a pair of very high and very delicate strappy gold sandals. The straps are so thin it looks as if I have gold lace on my feet. The straps crisscross my feet and continue up my calves. I don the shoes as a way to entice you. I know you love women in sexy shoes.

The outfit is beautiful and seductive. You can clearly see my naked body under the sheer red silk; the gold threads sparkle in the candlelight and are accented by the filigree gold heels.

I look in the mirror. I look freshly fucked. My face and skin glow with recent sex, my hair is tousled, and my scent of sex is noticeable.

'Who could be here that he would want to me to join them dressed so seductively?'

'My surprise.'

As if you were reading my thoughts, you call to me to join you. I walk out, unsure of whom I might meet in such a state of undress. You are lounging in your living room with a young man, drinks in hand. You both rise when I enter. You walk over and kiss me very passionately, and then whispering, "you look so beautiful." I smile. You always know what to say.

Turning towards your/our guest you introduce me to Nathan, a young college kid you met at the gym.

My mind starts ticking away; my mind is almost always ticking. Nathan is noticeably uncomfortable; I glance quickly at his crotch and see the outline of a partial erection as he is extending to shake my hand.

Wild thoughts race through my head and I glance at you and your devilish grin. My eyes and my smile let you know I'm going to enjoy this surprise very much, you devil.

You hand me a cocktail and another to Nathan.

Nathan is barely legal, just started college, shy, tall, blonde hair, and no noticeable body hair. He has a swimmer's body; long, lean, and muscular. His face is that of a cute boy emerging into a man.

We sit, and I think, 'this is going to be fun.'

I'm a bit wicked in a fun, sexual way. I'm not sure what you were planning, lover, but I suspect this young Adonis is my surprise… and I plan to seduce, teach, and enjoy his young, eager, virginal body.

Oh yes, this will be very fun.

I purposely sit where Nathan must look at me. Sitting with the robe completely wrapped, with my large tits still clearly visible… he is so adorable, trying not to be obvious but still looking at them. I make it easy for him; I lean back and extend my body so that all of my nakedness can be seen through the red cloth. We chat, we laugh, I flash you both…Sharon Stone style…from time to time. It is obvious by my scent that I'm excited and you comment on it.

"Do you smell that Nathan? That is the most wonderful smell in the world. That is the smell of excited pussy."

Lover, you are a devil.

Nathan smiles, noticeably red in the face, but happy to learn. Feeling bold, I open my legs wide.

And say, "and this is what an excited pussy looks like."

Nathan looks, and then looks at you, and again back at me.

"Do you want to look closer?"

"Do you want to touch it?" I ask.

You chime in, "You should taste it."

Nathan stands and makes no effort to hide his erection, comes over and sits on the floor in front of my snatch. He is staring so intently, like an examination.

I lie back and open my legs even wider, and I feel my lips spread for him.

You walk over and sit next to Nathan.

The lesson begins.

You point out key sensitive areas. You glide his hand, fingers, over my body, my breasts, into my pussy and rubbing my clit. Together, you and Nathan finger me to orgasm. You share your masterful skills and knowledge on how to please this woman. And Nathan is a quick learner.

I love the attention, both of you caressing me. Two beautiful men loving my body...I lie back and enjoy.

You glide his fingers in my openings, first fucking my pussy and then my ass with his fingers. You know I love it; I make no effort to hide my pleasure.

You reiterate to your pupil the importance of pleasing the woman first. So many men don't know anything about female sexuality. I believe you are making the world a better place by helping this young man and making my night one to remember.

First lesson complete. I'm lying in bliss from all the attention. My pussy is glistening. The room smells of sex. My sex.

Having had several orgasms since the evening started, now I really want to be fucked. I want you to get on top and pound into me so hard that the sound of our skin crashing makes an audible 'slap,' your hardness ramming me, pushing my body and the sofa across the floor.

You know I want this; with each orgasm comes a greater physical yearning to be filled. I need your cock in me. I want your weight pressing down on me. I want your entire body compressing the air out of my lungs as you grind into my sex. Grab my legs by the ankles and open me wider and just fuck me!

But I know this kind of aggressive fucking would frighten our little lamb, so I let you direct the show. I am willing to play by the rules, teacher.

Leaning over my pussy, and in what seems to be mere seconds, you lick and suck my clit and I come again.

Nathan watches in amazement. I moan in pleasure.

I love how skilled you are. I'm addicted to your tongue.

"I'll teach you all about that later. Right now we need to get you some relief. Your dick is so hard it has to hurt."

That is my cue; I know it without you even telling me.

I join you and Nathan on the floor. I take charge and move in to kiss Nathan. I ask him has he kissed a girl before?

"Yes," he says.

I ask, "Have you made out for hours, rubbed your bodies together until you came with your clothes on?"

"How do you do that?" was his response.

I think, 'Oh lover, I love my surprise, he is so beautiful, eager, and adorable. And I think of the good we are doing for this young buck to take into the world. His future lovers will be so grateful.

I lie down next to Nathan, and pull him to me. Facing each other we begin to kiss, slowly at first, and then more passionately. I glide my hands along his body and then in turn glide his along mine. I wrap my top leg around his butt and pull his groin into mine.

I start very slowly to grind into him; he feels the rhythm and joins me in the dance.

We are making out and dry humping, except I'm mostly naked. I have the red robe on, but my body is completely exposed…only my arms are covered. Even with this scant bit of clothing, combined with the CFM shoes, my body feels decorated.

I feel his cock, so hard. I don't think he will last much longer. I have my hands up under his shirt…his chest is so smooth…then down his pants. His ass is so tight. He is physical perfection.

You join us on the floor. You've discarded your pants and saddle up behind me, pressing your cock against my ass. I moan. Your cock always excites me. You wrap your arms around me to play with my tits while kissing the back of my neck. I'm in sex heaven. You grind your cock into my ass, as I grind my pussy into Nathan's cock, creating a very erotic rhythm.

I'm sandwiched between two beautiful men, both adoring my body, four hands, two mouths, two cocks.

'Lover, I love my surprise!'

As I had suspected, our student has reached his maximum. With great gusto he cries out and I can feel through his jeans his dick release. His mouth moves away from mine, and his head falls back as his hands grab my ass, pulling me against his cock.

A few moments pass, he is quiet. I whisper, "Do you feel good?"

"INCREDIBLE!" he states.

"I didn't know I could cum with my clothes on."

"Should I be embarrassed for coming so soon?"

"I couldn't help it.."

Nathan is so adorable. His shyness has eased and is replaced by eager curiosity. I'm enjoying his non-stop questions. He feels safe.

There is no judgment. He is glowing from his first real sexual experience.

I now take this time to do what I have wanted to do since I walked in at eight, (excuse me, five to eight, because I was not late this time).

I roll you on your back. You smile. You know what is coming. You know what I love, crave, and need. Your dick is beautiful and pointing straight up in the air. It is hard and thick and the veins are engorged along the shaft. Your knob is so enlarged that a little precum has seeped out.

You are so beautiful, lover. I let my eyes drink up your maleness. A work of art!

I bring my head down to collect the dew off the tip. I love your taste. My eyelids drop, I'm in a trance, you know this about me. I want your hardness to stretch out the side of my cheeks. I want to feel your cock hit the back of my throat.

Often I will play, bring you to the edge and back away. Building the tension. Prolonging our pleasure. But now several hours have passed since I arrived, and I want you. I want it hard, I want it rough. I want your cum.

I slide my lips over the tip down the shaft, all the way to the base. I go deep; you let out a smiling moan. You have been smiling all night, you devil. Nathan watches intently. You know he is watching. This excites both of us. I feel your girth grow just a touch, stretching my lips a bit wider, and your cock twitches involuntarily with excitement.

You will not last long. We both know it. Which is perfect since I'm sure you have more planned. But it is time for you to receive, and I love to give.

Nathan's shyness is now gone. He is verbalizing his commentary.

"Oh god! You both look so hot."

"I might cum from watching."

He takes off his clothes and starts rubbing himself while watching me mouth-fuck you.

You tell him not to cum, he will be next. Knowing I will love sucking this pretty boy's dick.

I return my focus to you. I can tell you want it rough as well. You weave your fingers though my hair, pulling my head down deeper on you. I slide my tongue and mouth up and down. Covering my teeth with my lips, I apply more pressure to the shaft and progressively more speed, pistoning my hand, tongue, and mouth up and down. I slip my other hand down to cup your balls, massaging them lightly. You moan—I know this familiar sound of pleasure… you are so close. I feel it in your balls, and in my mouth. Your knob swells…seconds away.

I slide my hand down lower and apply pressure to your anus, rimming the edge as your pelvis raises up to meet my mouth. God I love the feeling of you fucking my mouth. As you are shooting hard down my throat, Nathan gasps. You smile, and I smile with lips shiny from your cum.

I lie on top of you. We kiss. "I love my surprise."

I move off you, we both look at Nathan with his hard dick bobbling in the air. He's an eager puppy.

You look at him.

"You ready for the best blow job of your life?"

He nods yes.

I lay him down.

You watch as I slowly begin to make love to this young virgin. He is physically flawless, steeped in the beauty of youth.

I begin by kissing his belly. Slowly I move around his belly button and then very slowly moving down to his sex hair. I breathe on his cock, he moans. I must be careful. He could come quickly, and I want to savor him.

I lightly lick up the length of his shaft. He moans louder.

His dick is so lovely. It is thinner than yours but long and smooth with a fat head on top. His balls are nearly hairless, and on the sides is a nice patch of dark blonde sex hair.

Nathan is clearly enjoying my proclivity for BJs and between strokes I whisper how much I love a hard cock in my mouth.

You move to the floor next to Nathan. I'm licking the underside of Nathan's cock then gently rolling his balls in my mouth.

You come up next to his penis, placing your hand on his dick and gently gliding his cock back to my mouth. Then you begin to kiss my lips, with his dick in my mouth. I take him all in, deep down my throat. He moans and gasps at the same time. He has dreamed… fantasized, but never in his young life realized how incredible this would feel.

I feel his cock grow substantially in my mouth. He will not last long. He is young and inexperienced. The feeling of having his cock licked, tongued, and sucked is so new and wonderful. His body is joyfully reacting to these novel sensual sensations. I love it. I love his enthusiasm. He is enjoying me enjoying him. The way sex should be.

I slide up and down letting my tongue circle the head each time I rise to the top. His body goes tense, and his legs tighten up, his ass contracts. He is seconds away.

You have been watching from the start, brushing my hair from my face, nibbling on my breasts, my neck, kissing my mouth as I slide up and down Nathan's dick.

He's about to explode. I slide up to the tip and stop for a second to prolong the pleasure.

You come in and lick the tip.

I'm fascinated.

Your tongue on his cock excites me. I lean in to kiss you and we begin to kiss, deep tongue kisses while sharing Nathan's cock in our mouths.

Nathan moans.

I reach around your head and pull you deep into my mouth while pushing our lips together tightly. I glide you down his cock. We stroke his virgin dick with our mouths and tongues. Up and down, you moan, I'm so wet I think I will come, and then Nathan explodes with pleasure. We hold the pressure while sucking on him. His sweet cum begins to pour out of our mouths. We try to catch it all, but some slips past our lips. We continue to kiss his pretty cock with his warm sweet cum shared between us.

Nathan is momentarily spent. He is lying on his back in relaxed bliss. You and I, however…the fire is just getting started.

We continue to kiss, our lips and tongues hungry for more. Soon our bodies are tangled together, arms and legs wrapped around each other, pulling our bodies closer as our lips remain connected. For a few minutes we forget our guest.

Our minds and bodies are one. We are connected in all ways possible as you slide into me. Nirvana! I feel you in me, solid, hard, and wonderful.

Our bodies move in a rhythm we both know, as we continue to kiss.

At this moment, Nathan sits up and begins to watch; our spell is broken. My 'surprise' wants more. All shyness is gone and the happy puppy is ready to play some more.

With one last thrust you push yourself, so hard I feel it from the inside out. Pure physical excitement rushes over my body. You pull out leaving my body empty and wanting.

You smile and look at me, "Now my dear…show our guest heaven."

You devil. I'll ride this man-boy. I'll enjoy every part of his perfect body. I'll do it, while you watch.

I slide next to Nathan. We share a kiss, a lovely passionate kiss with less urgency than initially. I know where this is going, no need to rush. With our lips locked I begin to stroke him. He is hard. Got to love youth, they are always ready. I smile while I think this.

I roll Nathan to his back. He is open, letting me direct him. We continue to kiss. I straddle him. My pretty red robe is really nothing more than a shawl now as it drapes over my forearms and across the small of my back. With feet still in the strappy gold heels resting on both sides of his thighs. I raise myself up and slide him into me. He feels good, really good.

I turn to look at you and smile. I mouth, "thank you, lover." You smile. You knew I would love having this young man. He is my first virgin. Nathan moans again, very low and earthy. He is going to enjoy what comes next.

I slowly grind my hips into him, he moans again. I circle my hips counterclockwise while sliding up and down his pole. I start slow so he can pick up the rhythm. His first few attempts to move with me cause him to slip out of my warmth. With no change in my rhythm I slide him back in, and each time he moans, sounds of ecstasy.

His eager young cock is delicious. I continue to lead and he begins to follow. I increase the intensity, moving a little farther in and a little harder. I flex my muscles around his shaft and he lets out a sound of thrilled surprise.

I begin to feel myself close, again, and I know Nathan will explode shortly. I look at you and move one hand behind me to cup his balls and the other to finger myself. Both Nathan and I respond to this added stimulation with a deep moan. I look over, and you are so hard. I want you in my mouth.

You stroke yourself a bit just to tease me.

I feel myself losing control. I speed up the rhythm for my own satisfaction. Nathan follows beautifully, a quick study, our boy.

Then it hits; each enormous wave of pleasure begins to take over my body…I feel it deep in my core, my head rocks back, I arch my back, and thrust down as hard as I can. At the same time Nathan is pushing into me; I can see by the distorted anguish on his face he is coming as well. He quietly screams. I whimper and moan and I can see you are smiling.

I collapse on his chest. After a few minutes I rise up and lightly begin to kiss his lips, his face. His eyes are closed savoring his first time.

We stay like this until he slides out of me.

I then roll over on my back next to him.

You and I are now lying on each side of him. He is relaxed and blissful. We together caress this young man with our hands, and then lips. He accepts our affection without movement. He tells us how amazing he feels, we both smile.

Our beautiful man-boy falls into a deep and peaceful sleep. We let him rest. Our lips find each other and we begin our dance.

I want to physically thank you for sharing and giving me such a delightful 'surprise.' I would have never thought something so erotically fun would happen to me. But you made it happen. You make everything good happen. Thank you, lover, for finding this beautiful virgin. His first time will be forever one of my favorite experiences.

We continue to kiss; the passion and heat between our bodies builds. You move your lips to my neck. I love this. You move down my body until your lips reach my opening. You breathe in deep, enjoying my scent and the aromas of sex lingering between my legs. You dive in. I always welcome your tongue.

You lick and suck all of me…my juice and Nathan's. You drive me to the edge with your crazed hunger for my pussy. I ride your tongue and you only come back harder. We are manic and noisy, and still our young boy-man sleeps like an angel.

Our bodies part long enough for us to make it back to your bed.

Finally, baby, after countless orgasms, you give me some good old fashioned fucking, missionary style. I know tonight has turned you on as much as me. You waited your turn, until I wore out my surprise, as we knew I would. Very few have my endurance for sex. You know this about me.

You crash down in me hard and fast. I want you this way and you know it. You smile as you pound me harder and harder…it turns you on to be so dominant after so many hours of being in a passive, submissive role.

You grab my wrists with your hands and move them over my head, pinning me to the bed, and continue to fuck me. I can't help but gasp each time you push a little harder into me. I love your hard cock and I can feel it getting harder. Lover, fuck me, slam your whole body into me, I love it. Sweat begins to run down the sides of your face; you are working. I love sweat with a purpose.

You fuck me so hard you've literally beaten another orgasm out of me. I'm coming, and you know it. There's no denying as my body nearly levitates off the bed, I want you to know you did this to me; you gave me this much pleasure. I want you to feel all of it. I want you to see, feel, smell, and hear my body responding to you.

The pure expression of my passion finally pushes you over, and you gush in me. I begin to feel you, enjoying me, enjoying you. You cry out in pleasure.

I live to hear this sound from you.

You bring yourself down and rest yourhead next to mine. For minutes we are breathless. Sex like this leaves us both speechless.

No need to talk. We both know this was an incredible evening. Lover, I love your surprises.

In what feels like just a few minutes later, I am awakened by the lovely sensation of Nathan kissing my right breast. Our Adonis is awake and I think he's hungry.

It's morning, light seeps into the room through the curtains.

His beautiful blonde hair is so soft as I stroke it. This activity awakens you, my sweet. You look over and begin to suck on my other tit. I lie there enjoying and marveling in my good fortune, two gorgeous men, making love to me.

Slowly both of you continue to enjoy licking, sucking, kissing me all over. This has to be heaven.

Nathan, I can see is very hard. I reach over and stroke him. He moans. It's so sweet. It's all so new to him, and the pleasure for him is so real and untarnished. I enjoy my new toy. I look at you with a look of gratitude.

This morning you boys-men make me feel like a goddess. I just lie back and relish. You both kiss my neck, my breasts, and both feet at the same time. It's lovemaking being mirrored in stereo... very arousing. Seems Nathan has a thing for feet as well. You probably knew this already.

Just like you, he likes it all. Each of you tickling my toes with your tongues; it's unbelievable. Then he wants to try...what he's never tried. He's a bit afraid, intimidated and unsure. He wants to eat my pussy. First you, then him, taking turns. He could have no better teacher. You are the master.

I'm a very fortunate girl. This is sex heaven.

When he feels confident, you both delve in, two tongues together kissing me so intimately. I can't help myself; I lie there and cum again and then again and then again. I just keep flooding your mouths. I'm intoxicated with pleasure. You two are quite a team.

At some point when Nathan comes up for air, I pull him to my mouth; we kiss ferociously. Our boy is getting into the spirit of things. We continue to make out as you continue to lick me. Truly no one is better at this than you.

I stroke his body; he is so hard. He won't last much longer. And really, who can blame him. In less than 12 hours he's gone from being a virgin to trying a number of erotic activities many adults haven't ever allowed themselves to enjoy.

He shyly whispers in my ear "Can I come in you again?"

I smile. He is just too adorable, too perfect for words. I continue to stroke him.

I answer, "of course, you can do anything you like."

He smiles so big, like he got a new red bike for Christmas.

"Can I try fucking you from behind like in the porno movies I've seen?"

I laugh out loud; he is momentarily afraid he did something wrong. I assure him he did not.

I share with you his request and you chuckle a little as well.

Ah lover, our boy is growing up so fast.

I kiss him hard and lovingly to let him know it's all okay. He can say whatever he likes. There is no judgment and no rules.

I position myself on all fours on the bed, and he comes up from behind. Not really sure of how to 'mount me' I glide his dick into me. Wow, he's so hard.

Since he is not exactly sure of how to proceed, I start to rock myself into him. He quickly picks up the rhythm and he begins to really enjoy himself. He gasps and moans as we pick up the tempo.

He feels so nice.

You are sitting on the bed in front of me watching. You are so hard. I'm staring at your cock, willing it into my mouth.

I think you finally sense my desire for you and you move forward so I can suck on you as Nathan fucks me from behind. You continue to watch and I continue to enjoy. I can't believe how good it feels to have you both in me together, like a sex goddess.

Nathan cries out and comes. I could feel him close and I tighten up around him. He falls on to me, hugging me from behind. I continue with you.

Knowing you and mornings, I know you are not far from coming. The feel of your engorged dick in my mouth is better than coffee. I speed up the pace because I know you want to come. You shoot hard, gushing your seed down my throat. I continue to suck until you are soft. We are all relaxed.

Nathan looks at the clock,

"I don't want to go, this has been the best night of my life."

I tell him, "it was…it was an amazing night."

I invite him to stay for breakfast, but he kisses me very tenderly and runs out the door, "I'm late for class."

I invite our young lover back, but I'm not sure he heard me.

Then I turn to you, you are smiling that devilish smile, and I crawl up to meet your lips.

"I loved my surprise! You are simply beyond words!"

We start to kiss; it's time for the adults to play.

EMBERS

Do you believe in sexual healing?

*W*E HAD BEEN FIGHTING IN A SENSE, SAME FIGHT AS ALWAYS. I want more, and you can't give more. I think it's over. Again. But like a moth to a flame, I can't resist the light…it feels too good. I'm not alone in this emotional dance; you are drawn to me too.

We meet, I don't know what to expect, but like always, awkwardness turns into familiarity that turns into fun. We connect…we just do…on many levels.

We close the bar. You walk me to my car. Will you kiss me? I hope so. I always want you to kiss me. With you, I never know how it will end.

You get in my car, I don't know how it starts, but it does.

You mention wanting to fuck me in the back seat, and without hesitation I lower the seats, doff my jeans, and present my pussy for you to fuck. I don't even know how you folded yourself in a position to fuck in such a cramped spot, but we are fucking in a very well-lit parking garage, and I don't care. My only concern is that you don't stop, not ever. Fucking like randy teenagers who don't have access to a proper place to fuck, we fuck. It is manic and sexy and probably illegal. But I have always enjoyed the thrill of public places and I love the thrill of you every time you enter me.

It was so hot…even now it sends desire through my body for you.

There are several other places I would love to break public decency codes. You wanna break the law?

I'M IN A HURRY. I'M ALWAYS IN A HURRY.

Running to Starbucks: I promised the girls in the office coffees.

Blended things I can't pronounce.

I see you before you see me.

Decide to test a theory and hopefully put it into practice.

"Can a woman just ask? And make it happen?"

I sit at your table.

"Hello."

Whisper something about "want some?"

I gesture by slowly rolling my head and eyes towards the bathroom, indicating direction/location.

I get up and move in that direction, you follow.

Inside, lights on,

"Click"

Door locks.

Mouths. Tongues, hands everywhere. Clothes land on the floor. It's manic, frantic and rushed,

You push our bodies against the wall; I slide down to suck you.

You are very hard. I like that.

I know I'm wet.

You flip me over, leaning me over the sink, and enter from behind,

I arch my back and push back to meet you. I'm watching you in the mirror.

You're watching you enter me.

It's hard, fast, deep, and raw.

This is fucking/screwing/boning.

No foreplay. No prologue. No time.

We can hear the milk foaming outside.

I'm very awake now, no coffee needed.

Brief salutations. I'm late.

Too bad for the girls at work, no coffee. I'll buy them lunch instead…unless you happen to be at Subway.

I'M IN A WEIRD MOOD.

It's easy for me to write to you because I know you won't answer.

I feel restless.

I feel raw and exposed as if my skin has peeled back off my flesh.

I know why people drink: so they can dull this feeling rather living with it.

It's not just pain. It is the constant discomfort.

I wish it would pass, but then I'm afraid it will.

Leaving me feeling nothing.

I wish, but I don't know what I wish for.

I want, but I don't know what I want.

It doesn't really matter. Whatever I say I want will not be what I want once I get it. I am never satisfied, a blessing and a curse.

I feel hungry, always needing and wanting more.

Why am I never ever satisfied?

Why can't I be happy?

I have so much and yet I want more, always more! I feel greedy, despite what I want not being material possessions.

Most of all, I need to feel alive.

I want to feel you.

Where are you, my love?

Why did you leave?

*Y*OU CALL. IT'S LATE.
It's always late.

"Nightcap?"

You know the answer to that, without asking.

I'm not sure if I should feel good that you think of me in these late hours, or worry.

I'm not worthy of daytime thoughts?

Either way, you are my weakness.

You know this.

You call, I answer.

I always respond.

Why do I answer?

The flesh is weak, and yours feels too good.

SOMETIMES IN THE QUIETNESS OF MY MIND, WHEN NO OTHER thoughts are barging in and taking over present consciousness, I escape to my fantasyland. If I concentrate and search the cortex of my brain, I can find the place that brings me to you.

I feel your lips on mine that first time, so surprising There was so much longing and pent up desire.

How long had I wished it? Years?

I only wish I could burn this memory and feeling into my brain to enjoy over and over again.

I close my eyes and your lips are there on mine. I move to bring my body closer to yours.

I think for a second that I'm acting too eager. Funny, I remember having this thought. I backed away, let you come to me, and you did.

My attempt at distance lasted seconds. I wanted you. And you wanted me too.

Why make any pretense about it? Lust, longing, and finally… sex. Finally!

The weight of your body on mine, nirvana!

Our desire lined up together, fully clothed, but I could feel you as if we were naked. Clothes did not hinder the passion.

Sometimes when you desire water and you finally get it, your thirst is satisfied.

I finally got that drink of water, but in your absence the thirst remains, even stronger.

The reality of you made the desire more. Never in my life has anyone made me want like you do. I want you, but not in some conventional way. I don't want to be involved day to day. I want you, nonetheless. I want you the way people desire vacations: it's not about day-to-day life but the wonderful, blissful times in between the drudgery of everyday.

The holiday I visit in my mind today is the circle of 69, a favorite of yours. I adore your enthusiasm for wanting me to feel as good or better than you.

Do you sex vacation in your mind as well?

*F*OND MEMORY.

I like when you lace your fingers through my hair and gently, yet with urgency, glide my head and mouth in closer to your cock.

Direct me to feel all of you in my mouth, the head hitting the back of my throat.

The turgid pressure increases, and your beautiful cock grows even fatter.

My mouth can sense the change.

You push me in a little deeper.

I like this. I crave it!

Your legs and ass muscles tighten and I know we are close.

*A*T TIMES WHEN MY CLIENTS ARE DRONING ON AND ON ABOUT whatever, I find my mind will slip for a few seconds to the exquisite pleasure of your tongue thrumming my clit, and your fingers penetrating my slit. The memory of this hypnotic pleasure is overwhelming, and I can feel the blush in my cheeks. It would be embarrassing if anyone knew what flashed through my thoughts.

Some men are so afraid or maybe bewildered by the most intimate and naturally erogenous parts of a woman's body. I have always felt the boys who are obsessed with breasts to be just babies. Men, grown men, know to move lower, to the epicenter of lust and desire.

Sadly, it seems, I…like many women…meet too few men who can unleash the fire, who welcome it. We (collectively) are so grateful when men get it right.

Men, in my experience, are often selfish takers of pleasure. Equating their own pleasure as being satisfying to their partner, they are not nurturers. Women are more often givers. They will sacrifice their own pleasure for a man in hopes of receiving his gratitude as love or some other future wish that, sadly, is rarely fulfilled

Men just don't think that way. Pleasure now. Women hope for the future. Sacrifice now for security later.

What men should learn is if they gave just a little, women would give so much more. And this is the person you want. She is uninhibited, fully sexual, exciting, unpredictable, and hedonistic.

Men accuse women of not being interested in sex. More likely, it's that they are conditioned to expect so little from the act of sex that enthusiasm is sparse, since there will be no real satisfaction. Frustration at the most primal level, unmet lust is her "reward." It becomes a lot of effort for very little return. A nap, shopping, or chocolate provide more satisfaction and fulfillment.

But this day, I have an undeniable physical response to the images of the sensations created by you in my mind. I feel a rolling wave of heat, deep, very deep in my core from my navel to my knees.

I feel weak in my legs, yet strong and alive. I am flushed, warm, and wet, and getting wetter as I let the images linger in my mind.

I wonder if my excitement shows. I feel like an exposed wire and just a few more moments of these delicious thoughts might just push me to the edge.

I'm so highly aroused that I absolutely must get some relief. At lunch I'll go and get myself off. It seems to be the only way I will make it through the day. But really, it's only a bandage. What I need is to be pounded deeply: I need to get fucked; I need to be filled.

I need you.

SMOLDERING

Choose me.

*"G*IRL, YOU KNOW I WANT YOUR LOVE!
    Your love was handmade for somebody like me

Come on now, follow my lead… "

It's a popular song, and it has been playing on the radio for over two years. I think the music industry purposely overplays songs until we think we like them, when really it is just familiarity we interpret as liking. Hearing this song is personal torture.

We are in your kitchen, arriving home from someplace. You are chastising Alexa to play something you want to hear. You make each of us a drink; most likely we don't need another. This song comes on, and you begin to sing. I love when you sing. You even dance a little. I love that too. Free expression of happiness takes you over and it makes me love you more in that moment. You bring me the glass of whiskey…it is always whiskey with us, with one big ice cube. As you hand me the glass, you circle your arm around by your waist: in professional dance this move would be called a samba roll, but in the club it is booty grinding. By any name, I love it. Sexy dancing in your kitchen is the perfect way to end the evening.

"I'm in love with the shape of you
We push and pull like magnets do

Although my heart is falling too

I'm in love with your body

Last night you were in my room…"

The dancing slow grind continues as you slip your fingers up inside me, something you rarely do anymore a surprise I love. You kiss the back of my neck as you finger fuck me. I put the drink down on the kitchen table…things are heating up.

"And now my bed sheets smell like you"

This overplayed song brings me back to our sexy dance in your kitchen. A sexy memory that makes me miss you even more.

"I'm in love with your body."

I WISH I COULD KISS YOU.
I love kissing.

We both enjoy this love art form.

Often neglected because fucking seems to be what really matters most of the time…

But right now, I just want to feel your lips on mine. Ever so lightly let our mouths meet, lips part, soft and lovely.

Our bodies barely press together just enough to feel the electricity: our lips still connected and every so often our tongues dancing around each other.

This is my wish for right now.

Are you wishing for my lips too?

"*I* WANT YOU…TO WANT ME.
 I need you…to need me.

I'd love you…to love me.

I'm begging you…to beg me"

I always thought of this as a stupid song by a mediocre 70's band, until you.

The song is pop, displaying no real depth or complexity.

But the words…ah, the words…are of longing.

The longing I understand.

I know you want me, but not like I want you.

I know you don't need me, and I don't need you.

But need has nothing to do with affairs of the heart.

I know you love me, but not like I love you.

Furthermore, my way of loving is not what you want.

Your way of loving leaves me full of self-doubt.

I wish you would beg me, but begging is not your style.

And I've begged already.

Is it better to have unfulfilling love or no love?

It is not your fault or mine that our love styles are not the same.

You love in a worldly way, letting the universe carry you to wherever and whenever our paths may cross. It's airy and free.

You sprinkle love on me when the mood strikes.

I love in an earthy, homey way. I hold what I love close and constant.

I supply love more like a blanket of warmth.

Your love leaves me wanting, needing and begging.

Your torture is not deliberate, but it is real.

You must be my muse.

You supply so much pleasure when I'm in your presence and then so much pain in your absence. It leaves me questioning everything I believe and desire. My body aches for your touch. I need to love you. I feel withdrawal when I must endure without you, my love.

Our sexual intensity is explosively charged, which is exciting… but it also drains my energy.

The combustion of explosives leaves only the aftermath debris.

Extreme sexual attraction that verges on obsession, maybe it's only me, but I don't think so, my love.

The magnetic pull is difficult to control or even comprehend.

I feel mesmerized.

It leaves me weak, confused, and isolated when you are not there.

Your cock is the cure.

But at what price, my dignity? My well-being? My soul?

I miss you.

*H*URT
     Anger

Heartbreak

"Why are you here?"

Audacity!

Dive bar

Tears

Drinks

More drinks

More tears

Sadness

Door locks

I squat, you unzip

Hard in my mouth

Sleazy bar bathroom

I stand, you bend me over

We hate fuck

It's hot, so hot!

The end.

Again.

*F*OR MONTHS I MADE SURE I WAS "FUCK READY" AT ANY GIVEN moment. (Today may be the day he calls. Need to be ready.) Since our meetings are always impromptu, like a good horny girl scout I always want to be prepared. Legs shaved, pussy manicured in the fashion that you like, and sexy underwear...all for you. Sadly, you never call.

You stop calling. You leave me wanting and constantly on the verge of coming. This is the sorry fate of being the Plan B girl. I've never felt second-rate with you until now but I knew. I knew I was the intermission girl, the one before the next, newer occupation of your time, mind, and sexual desire.

Maybe we are not done. Maybe it's just a hiatus. Either way, it makes me sad. I wish we could play forever.

Why did we stop?

It's always your call, never mine: I never gave you any rules to adhere to

I accepted I was "Plan B girl." The girl you call when there are no others. It's odd that I would accept this arrangement, but I did. I think it's because you have never made me feel "second" when we are together. With you I only felt happy, sexy, and desired. I miss your presence. When you withdraw, it takes away sunshine in my life.

I will masturbate for weeks about your cock in my mouth...a pleasure I could never get enough of. I feel withdrawal, and like a bit of my heart will be scarred once again by you...until I can almost get through the day without thinking of you or your cock... and then you will appear again.

I will be cool but receptive until you and your cock weasel back into my life and my pussy. Bringing the joy back...and then the cycle will repeat.

Forever your Plan B girl.

E STRONG. BE STRONG. BE STRONG.

    I repeat it over and over in my brain.

You make me weak.

Why did I agree to meet you?

I feel empowered, and then I see you and my strength slips away.

Be strong.

I see you, you see me.

Your arms are up in the air as if you are cheering the sky at my appearance. I can see your smile. You make me smile. A little power has slipped away.

But I'm still strong.

You greet me with a warm hug and a kiss, as if nothing hs changed and no time has passed.

I reciprocate in equal fashion.

I am happy to see you.

Damn me.

Dinner is, as always, fun, and silly, then serious, then laughing again. Being with you has never been hard. I enjoy you, and I think you enjoy me.

It's after dinner that is always the dilemma.

By dessert, your hands have caressed me. First my hands, then my face, to the small of my back, maybe even my breasts.

I love the attention.

I love your touch.

Furthermore, I love to touch you. I try…but I can't keep my hands off of you. I reach over to play with your hair, pat your belly…whatever whim strikes. I don't even try to restrain myself, it feels too nice.

Ah…but after dinner. We are walking to my car. Be strong, be strong, be strong!

I wonder, will you invite me to come over? I want you to want me, but I will not go. Not because I don't want to, I want to very much!

I want you, much more than you want me, forever the problem.

You make me weak.

I can't have just a little bit of you. You ration off your affections in small parcels, and I love big.

I always jump in with both feet. I want to give you everything until I leave nothing of myself. You want only small bits of love and you only give small bits of love, when you are in the mood.

And tonight you are in the mood.

I'm at my car. You kiss me.

Will this be it?

This will be easy. I will be strong.

You kiss me again. A little kissing will not hurt my resolve.

This time I give some back. I drop my purse and my hands move up to your neck and wrap firmly around your back.

I let my body press up against yours.

Oh yes, you are making me weaker. You are a drug and I want more.

My hands move to your chest, first over your shirt and then under. You do the same. Hands touching skin, you brush across my breasts. You like my breasts. I like you touching me. I like touching you.

Our kisses are deep now, mouths open wide, tongues making love; my desire is fierce.

I decline your invitation to come over. I may have declined, but that is not what my heart or body wanted! My only comfort is the knowledge that breaking my addiction to you will be easier if I remain strong.

Thankfully (and regretfully), you do not put forth a second invitation.

It would have been nearly impossible for me to say no, twice.

We stand in the street, cars passing by, and make love to each other, as much as decency (barely) allows

A passer-by even tells us to get a room.

We laugh. I couldn't agree more. But I must remain strong.

I slide my hand down your pants. You are naked underneath. Why must I love the feel of your body so much?

You are hard.

Good.

I'm glad to know you feel the heat as well. I'm excited too.

Kissing you makes me wet. And within moments, I can feel the deep wave of desire build deep in my loins. (What a stupid phrase, ("my loins".) This sexual desire is deep in the lowest chakra, hard to describe where, but when you feel it, it's as if a narcotic has been released in your system and you no longer care. You just want. The want is primal and sexual. Animalistic. And I want you, which is my problem. I want you too much, more than you want me.

But you keep kissing me. Normally you would have stopped this public display by now. But you just continue and I let you because the feel and taste of you are so delicious. I don't want to stop. I can feel your body wants as well. I want you to want me.

You like this game and I don't like games.

I would have let you undress me there in the street if you had tried. I would have unzipped you and taken you in my mouth right there if I thought you would let me. Like a street hooker with no shame, I would have sucked you for the world to see.

How can one person have so much power?

Your spell over me is a sweet curse. In your presence I'm in heaven, but your distance leaves me feeling cursed for loving you.

My only power is to be strong and not submit to your will, but oh, how I want to give in! However, I know the pain when you eventually leave would be too much to bear, again.

I drive away...happy I remained strong and yet so sad I couldn't let myself share my love with you. Regardless, I feel the pain of your absence.

"*I*T IS WHAT IT IS, THIS IS."

    This is one of your favorite sayings. I understand it, but I'm not fond of it.

This is our relationship, however.

I have no claim to you and you have none on me.

You like the freeness, but it makes my heart ache.

I long for you.

I crave you.

I want to feel you bite and pull on my nipples.

I need to touch you.

The physical withdrawals when I can't be with you are unbearable.

You don't feel the same, and that makes it worse.

I'm an adult. I played with fire and got burned.

But in the heat of passion, a person doesn't think of anything but the ecstasy. The repercussions seem irrelevant, pushing anything sensible out of my thoughts, succumbing to the lustful craving of the moment.

I remember when you longed more for me, than I for you. I liked that better.

You whittled away a spot for yourself into my heart, and on some level I hate you for that.

I was fine, before

I didn't need you or anyone…and there you were, slowly creeping into my inner heart's core. A place few ever get to be…and now you are there.

You ration love out in such small parcels, and this only leaves me feeling more longing…and no satisfaction.

Why do I allow this?

Why do I allow you to have such power over me? My mind tries to justify such silly, stupid behavior, but my heart and my body just want to feel you. I want you naked next to me. Let me breathe in your skin. I long for your nakedness lying next to me, awake and in sleep.

You are cruel.

Your indifference is worse than outright rejection. Rejection…I would know where I stand, but you give out just enough attention to make me think you love me as well. But you don't. Or, not in a way I need, or deserve to be loved.

Why do I allow this?

It's your skin. I think of your naked body and the feel of your skin touching mine, and the energy is unmistakable. It is so powerful, our need to touch each other. I know you feel this as well. So many thoughts race through my head. Why, with such a powerful draw, do you deny your need for me?

Is there another reason? My heart aches as my mind struggles to think of the possibilities.

My spell on you has ended, but your spell is more powerful.

Why did you do this to me?

Did you need another loyal devotee?

Do you not have enough women?

I never wanted to own you. But I need to feel like I matter to you.

I must stop.

Goodbye, my love.

I love you. I know you know this. I don't care that you know. I feel it, so I will say it. But your love does not enrich my life; your love takes. This is not the love I want.

How dare you say you love me, and yet you give nothing even close to love?

Goodbye, my love. It's time to heal my heart. Time to look for love that feeds my soul, rather than sucking the joy out of it. How I still long for your hands to run across my bare skin…I ache for your touch.

Kiss me!

Smother me with your body.

How I wish I could make you crave me again, like I crave you.

Trying harder will not make you love me.

You keep your love from me. Why…when I am open to receiving all of you and loving you back even harder?

Why does the pain have to be so painful?

Why do we love when it hurts when it ends?

Why do I not want to let go?

Why don't you love me?

I thought I had enough love for both of us. I can't do this anymore.

My love, good-bye.

$\mathcal{S}$O SAD WHEN YOUR MIND KNOWS IT'S OVER, BUT YOUR HEART IS not over it yet.

My heart aches. Which is silly. I knew it was nothing. I knew it was impossible, and it would never progress to anything. Yet, like all fools in the past and in the future, we rush into love or lust or the desire to be wanted and adored, even if we know it's probably a mistake.

It's impossible and stupid to start, but we blindly rush in, leading with desire and not sensible behaviors.

Somehow you made me feel something. Damn you. You made me feel adored.

It was magnetic. Like the stars and the planets that pull each other through the universe, we came together.

I allowed you to enter places in my head and heart I should have kept closed, places you should not have been allowed in, if you were only planning to stay for a short visit.

I have never felt so comfortable with a person so quickly, as if we had connected again after many lifetimes. So strong, so fast, it was pure magic.

I CAN'T HELP IT. THOUGHTS OF YOU STILL INVADE MY MIND. Quiet times, when I finger myself, images of you still flood my mind. The way you licked me still makes me ready for fucking all these months later. The way you would pull my hair and head back to kiss me. I have a physical addiction to you and the way you made me feel.

*T*HE ROOM WAS WHITE, ALL WHITE. THE CARPET, THE DRAPES, the walls, the marble pillars, the benches, and the sofas…all bright white. The chandeliers were the only things not white, and the crystal prisms are casting sparkles of rainbows along the walls, despite the only color visible being white.

This was a hidden room in a now defunct hotel. Only the top floors of this former beauty are used for a bar and restaurant.

We met for drinks, haven't seen you in months.

Why do you keep coming around when I clearly have let you go?

Why do I let you in, yet again?

Lovers have spent years, lifetimes, and centuries trying to figure this out.

Simple enough, the heart wants what the heart wants.

Logic, what's healthy, unhealthy, mistrust, pain, hurts, deception none of that matters to the heart, only to the brain. The heart aches for the love lost, it's just that simple.

But the rest is not simple.

We meet again, and again we connect, like we always do. I promised myself we would not end up in bed together, but I would kiss you if you tried to kiss me. I would not make the first move.

We sneak into this all-white room. It looks like a set from the movie "Eyes Wide Shut." It's dazzling, and slightly creepy at the same time.

I'm not sure of its purpose: maybe weddings, back in its heyday.

We walk around separately, checking out the space; we meet in the middle and begin to kiss, I don't know who started it, it just happened. And now that it happened, it can't stop. Neither of us tries to stop it.

Connected, we move to a room in the back of this maybe chapel. The back room is still white, but has red sofas. Who decorated this place?

You flip me over the back of the couch, raise my skirt, and enter me. It's dark in this room, just ambient light and the reflection of the large floor-to-ceiling mirror bearing witness to our fucking. It's crazy, I wasn't even going to kiss you, and now you are fucking me in this crazy room in this old hotel and I want nothing more than for you to never stop.

My body is screaming for you to fuck me harder. Leave nothing. Use all of me. Fuck me until I can't see, breathe, hear, or feel. It is only me and you in this moment.

But we both hear the door at the front open. Someone else has entered the white chamber.

We stop.

We leave.

You leave.

The heart wants what the heart wants; logic, decorum, and rules don't apply.

We stop again and I ache for more.

I miss you.

*L*IFE UNCHANGED IS DEATH. I'T'S DREARY THIS REBIRTH WITHOUT you as I watch the sunset I forever remember it all, my love. And as I watch the sunrise today, I know I will love again.

*I*T REALLY DOESN'T MATTER, LITTLE DOES IN THE GRAND SCHEME of things, but I miss touching you.

The feel of your skin on mine haunts my memory.

I know it sounds pathetic. It's been months and, really, I shouldn't feel like this still.

However, I close my eyes and I can still feel the warm exchange of your skin on mine.

Sometimes I can even conjure the feel of your body on mine. The memory of you is more like a snapshot rather than a complete recollection.

Your lips are on mine in a dream, a lovely dream that, sadly, continues to fade.

"*E*VERYTHING WILL BE ALL RIGHT IN THE END...IF IT'S NOT ALL right then it's not yet the end."

A favorite quote from a movie with a ridiculously long title!

So how does it end?...because these things are never *completely* over...

Love never ends. It just changes.

I changed. You did not.

I love you, God help me, I love you and the sex...my vagina starts to pulse just thinking about it. The memory of fucking you is something I will cherish until the day I die and beyond!

Your magical cock found the G spot...H I J K L M N O P!

I don't need a prince on a white horse, but I do need a man: A man who will cherish my heart as much as he cherishes licking my pussy.

Do I want too much? I don't think so.

If I can rock a man physically, emotionally, and mentally, I don't think love is too much to ask from my love.

I am hopeful...because, like fire, love never ends ... it transforms into something else that, eventually, brings about beautiful new growth.

KINDLING

Out of the ashes I rise again…
and I want… I want it all!

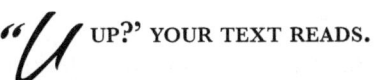
"*U* UP?' YOUR TEXT READS.

Modern technology is great, but it can lend itself to untraditional relationships.

I'm about to meet you in the flesh for the first time. So in reality, I don't know you. Oh, but I do know you, intimately.

I know your secrets and you know mine, shared via cyberspace.

Wonder if we don't even recognize each other?

I can sense creepiness, even through the Internet, so I believe we have a real connection, even in cyberspace.

How did it happen?

Not sure.

But it did not take long to reveal our secret desires. We have had sex many times via the web. Modern technology, strange and fascinating at the same time.

But tonight we meet.

I'm nervous and excited. I've wished on many occasions that we could meet for a glass of wine…have a normal conversation and flirt in person.

Wondering what your voice sounds like, what your hands feel like, what being with you will feel like. How you taste? The endless things I want to know about my secret lover.

Tonight we meet.

I know things about you few else know. I use this to my advantage. I wear a skirt…I'm usually in pants, but tonight I wear a skirt so you can see my shoes the moment I walk into the restaurant.

Plus, a skirt will be more advantageous for the other activities bound to take place.

I glance across the place; we spot each other at the same time. How silly to think we would not recognize each other.

You smile, big, and I can't help but smile back, big.

It's going to be a fun night.

You get up to greet me.

What will we do? Hug? Kiss?

It's a greeting for old friends and new lovers, very comfortable and nice.

I like you already, my friend.

You look down at my heels. I look down at your crotch. We laugh. We know tonight will be fun.

I agonized over how to dress my feet, knowing they would be a prominent feature tonight.

Red toes or deep pink? Red is always a good choice…just seemed too obvious. I went with a deep, dark pink.

Shoes, I love shoes, you love shoes. I own so many lovely pairs. But which pair will be perfect for my new lover? My foot lover, I will meet tonight.

I chose right, you tell me. Silver, strappy, very tall skinny heels with bling slung along the straps, jewels on my feet. They sparkle in the light. They are the star tonight.

You've ordered pink champagne. Perfect! I love champagne! Only fitting, you say, since we are celebrating. And we are.

Life is a celebration.

You are charming, smart, and handsome.

I'm still nervous but relaxed; we chat, we talk, we flirt, and we grow comfortable with each other in person. We converse like we have been friends for years. It's always magical when you meet someone who feels like they have always been part of your life, even though you've honestly just met.

The champagne does its magic. I feel sexy. You make me feel sexy. I start to reach over and stroke your arm as we talk…and then at times your thigh…and you do the same. You comment on my shoes, often. And what your plans are later for my shoes and toes. I smile. I want this too.

The meeting, the chatting, the champagne, the flirting…it's all foreplay, we know, but the anticipation is exciting. Why rush to the end, when the journey there can be so delicious?

Time passes in the restaurant, we are having fun…and we know more is going to happen soon.

I've begun to stroke the inside of your leg with my foot. First just the calf, then slowly moving up to your thigh. Boldly gliding my toes ever so quickly across your crotch. I feel the response from you instantly, and it shoots a fire of desire through me.

You look at me and we both know it's time. We walk toward the elevators; we are going to your room, nervous and excited. As the elevator doors close you press yourself against me firmly, letting me feel your excitement. You press all your body weight against me, and it fuels my excitement. We kiss for the first time, powerful and passionate but with delicate restraint, savoring the moment and building up the desire. I like kissing. It's so deeply sensual when done correctly.

Finally in your room…I have fantasized and masturbated so often about this it's hard to imagine I'm finally living the fantasy with you.

I'm reclined on the bed; you are kneeling on the floor at my feet. Your hands begin to massage my calves, my ankles, and you delicately plant whisper kisses on the tops of my feet. I'm already in heaven.

You remove my shoes and begin again with my naked feet. Sliding your thumb up the fleshy sole of my foot to the toes. Bliss! I dream it will never, ever stop.

Your lips replace your hands. You begin to kiss my feet, moving up the inside foot spine, working your mouth from the heel to the toes and back again…another level of ecstasy.

When I'm sure it's impossible to feel any more pleasure, you let your tongue slide along the arch of my foot, bringing your tongue in between my toes and then taking each one individually in your mouth and sucking them like little cocks. This alone might make me come.

I feel each kiss, lick, and suck on my toes at my clit. There must be a direct line. The pleasure is indescribable. Nothing in my life has ever felt so unexpectedly good. Each level of your lovemaking has exponentially added to my pleasure. I'm not hiding my enjoyment. I willingly accept this gift from you. My body heats up as gasps and moans escape from my mouth. You know what you are doing, and I am transformed by such a wildly erotic experience.

During the course of the massage and oral bath you gave my feet, you moved up on the bed. My skirt has moved above my thighs towards my waist. I've worn red lace panties that no longer completely cover my very swollen lips. I chose red because I knew you would like it.

I see you glance up and smile.

I wanted you to look. You can see everything through the lace. You can see my glossy pussy. You did this to me with your hands, mouth, and tongue on my feet.

The scent is faint, but you can smell my excitement, the perfume of my arousal.

Your mouth continues to worship my toes as your hands slide up and massage up my legs. You brush over my clit a few times just to heighten my arousal, teasing my body. Letting me know you are in charge and you know what you're redoing. In good time, I'll be begging you to let me come.

We move across the bed, oriented with my feet on your lap. It's finally my turn to give a bit of pleasure back to you.

My pink toes rub your cock through your trousers.

I feel you like it. And I like this too. You unzip, letting my feet feel just a bit more. Your cock hardens as my feet massage your shaft, your balls, and up to the tip again. In time, you finally remove the cloth barrier between your cock and my toes. You are now how I want you, naked. I so want to spin around and take you in my mouth, but not this time. This time is for my feet. And they are enjoying the starring role.

I slowly move from a playful massage to being more intent on increasing your pleasure. My feet are smooth and oiled up to allow easy gliding between the shaft and my toes. You create a tunnel with my soles to stroke yourself up and down. To create this position and to create this movement, my legs are wide open for you to look up at my glistening pussy.

It's my first time with foot lovemaking, but I sense you are enjoying my novice eager intentions. I know I'm incredibly turned on.

I have to come. I know I'm close. I have been close for hours, it seems. I reach down with my hand and push the soaked lace aside. I masturbate myself for you to watch while I continue to stroke your cock and you fuck my foot tunnel.

It's incredible…with every thrust of your cock between my feet, I feel like you have just pushed yourself deep into my vagina. I feel you in me, incredible!

I cum! I come hard! I shake. I arch way back, my head is now on the bed, my hand is still on my clit, my feet and your cock are still fucking, and I'm still coming. God, it feels like you are actually fucking me! What did you do to my feet? They are so sensitive to the pleasure.

Pleasure takes over you as well. I knew it was coming.

I could feel it in your balls, in your cock, on your face, in your breathing and your legs tensing up. I have wanted you to come since I walked into the restaurant.

I wanted to see the ecstasy on your face.

I wanted to know the smell of your cum.

I wanted to be with you in your moment of climax.

There's so much I want to learn about you, lover, and so much more to explore. You made my first time with you exhilarating.

My feet are now covered with the product of our passion.

I wonder if you will lick it off my feet? Or rub it on my feet and legs?

I can't wait to find out.

To be continued....